THE POWER
OF THE
GEMSTONES

CONFLICTING WORLDS

Written & Illustrated by Izzyanna Andersen

BEAVER'S POND
PRESS

BOOK 2

in *The Power of the Gemstones* series

ISBN 13: 978-1-59298-773-3

Library of Congress Catalog Number: 2018909864

Printed in the United States of America

First Printing: 2018

22 21 20 19 18   5 4 3 2 1

Book design and typesetting by Dan Pitts

BEAVER'S POND
PRESS

Beaver's Pond Press
7108 Ohms Lane
Edina, MN 55439–2129
(952) 829-8818
www.BeaversPondPress.com

To order, visit www.ItascaBooks.com
or call (952) 345-4488. Reseller discounts available.

For more information, visit www.thepowerofthegemstones.com or follow *The Power of the Gemstones* on Facebook.

THE POWER
OF THE
GEMSTONES

DRAGON TRIBES

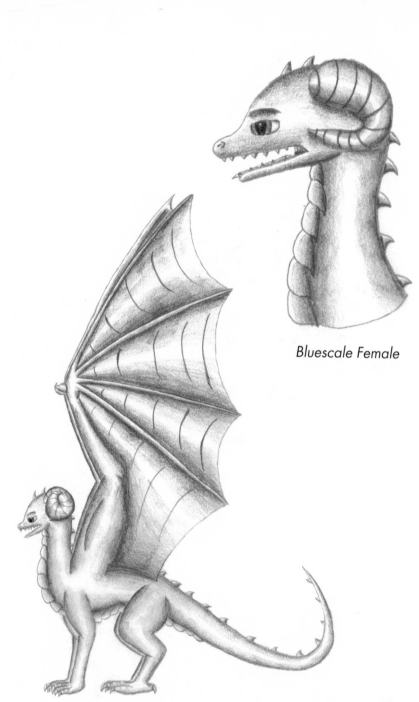

Bluescale Female

Bluescale Male

BLUESCALE DRAGON

Length: 20' – 30'
Height: 10' – 15'
Wingspan: 40' – 60', depending on length
and height of the Bluescale
Fire Power: Yes

Colors: The shiny scales of a Bluescale are varied shades of blue. However, color variations have occurred on occasion. Their talons, spikes, chest plates, wing undersides, and ram-like horns are all brilliant shades of yellow. Their small tongues are pink, with no fork at the end. The iris in a Bluescale's eye is normally a shade of blue, but variations have occurred at times.

Tribe Leader: Majesty

Details: Bluescales are a noble dragon tribe that lives in the Badlands of South Dakota, underneath the mountains within tunneling systems that both they and nature have created. Bluescales are omnivores, mainly eating meat from large mammals, but also eating bugs, fish, and even plants that grow within their land. Bluescales communicate verbally, as well as through telecommunication. Male Bluescales have larger horns and are slightly bigger than the females. Bluescales themselves are a stoic tribe that follows the rules of dragonkind. Though most seem cold at first, they protect whatever they care about most, whether for duty or their friends or family. They're even willing to lay down their lives should the worst happen.

Bloodclaw

BLOODCLAW DRAGON

Length: 20' – 60'
Height: 10' – 30'
Wingspan: 40' – 100'
Fire Power: Yes

Colors: Bloodclaws have blood-red scales with gray underscales. They have long, silver-gray horns and spines. The undersides of their wings are as black as the night. Their talons and forked tongues are a shiny black, and the eyes of a Bloodclaw are a glowing yellow.

Tribe Leader: Demonheart

Details: Bloodclaws are a violent, bloodthirsty tribe that lives deep within a hidden crevasse in Mystery Cave in Minnesota, deeper than any human has gone in the caves. The conditions in which they live are hot, crowded, smelly, and horrid. Bloodclaws are strictly carnivores, eating any kind of living creature, whether animals, the occasional human, dragons, or even their own kind. They speak jarred, confusing sentences almost no creature can understand, and they cannot telecommunicate. Bloodclaws are a dragon tribe with no empathy or common sense. They will strike and kill for the fun of it. If one should encounter a Bloodclaw, it is best to hide and pray for survival.

Pinescale

ADDITIONAL DRAGONS APPEARING:

PINESCALE

Length: 6' – 10'
Height: 3' – 5', 6' – 8' when standing on hind legs.
Wingspan: 12' – 20'
Fire Power: Yes

Colors: Pinescales have scales that are different shades of dark iridescent green. Their chest plates are lighter hues of green, and the scale-like spines on their backs are shades of brown. The undersides of their wings and their large, expressive frills are varying greens, and their talons range from colors of dark brown to black. A Pinescale's forked tongue is light pink, and their shiny, clever eyes are brown. Color variations do occur on occasion in Pinescales.

Tribe Leader: Sharptail

Details: Pinescales are a dragon tribe that lives within the trunks and branches of trees and underground burrows within the Superior National Forest. They are omnivores, eating everything from fish, mammals, and bugs, to plants, berries, and human food. They are capable of intellectual conversation and telecommunication, even using their frills and large scales as means of silent communication. They are one of the tribes with the smallest dragons. This does not make up for their personality or valor. Due to their heavy exposure to humans, Pinescales are masters at disguising themselves within trees and bushes and tricking humans. Though they are small, they are a close-knit tribe that expresses their emotions often and protects the ones they love.

PROLOGUE: CONFLICTS

When all is quiet, and all is perfect, all will stay together. But in the storms, in the conflicts, in the mighty battles of life, that is when you see who your true friends are; they will help you battle the storms.

Bella is not your ordinary thirteen-year-old girl.

She is, in fact, a Dralerian, a being that can transform from human to dragon because of the power of a gemstone. She fights alongside dragons known as Bluescales to try to end a war against the Bloodclaws, savage, bloodthirsty dragons. She is known as Emer to the Bluescales; she is a fierce warrior in their eyes.

But when Bloodclaws attacked the school Bella and her friends attended, she discovered that her friends were part of the Foretelling, words that predicted that four warriors, four Dralerians, thought to be extinct, would come to the dragons in their greatest time of need. They were the Chosen Ones.

However, troubles arose. When they first found out about her power, Bella's friends were furious that she hadn't told them about it. Bloodclaws attacked her and her friends. Demonheart, leader of the Bloodclaws, wanted to kill them all. But Bella and her friends stood strong, fighting and staying together to the end.

It has been four weeks since these events occurred. All has been silent, but not for long.

A new dragon, one thought to be dead by the Bluescales, has risen. As a secret assistant to Demonheart, he has made his orders clear. He will defeat Emer.

The Bloodclaws are stirring; the calm will soon become a storm.

Evil will attack again.

CHAPTER 1

WHEN YOU LOSE WHAT YOU LOVE

Today is the most important day of my life.

A young Bluescale walked down a stone tunnel, the tip of his pale-blue tail swishing slowly against the ground. His light-yellow talons clicked against the stone underneath him. His wings were folded neatly at his sides, and his head was held high.

Today is the day that I, Skye, become the apprentice to one of the highest-ranked guardians in the whole Bluescale cave.

As he walked, his eyes darted here and there, looking from every small niche and pebble around him to the large, mighty Bluescale in front of him. *Remember what Battlescar said,* Skye thought. *Analyze every detail. It will help you realize if something is wrong.* His eyes hovered on the navy-blue dragon in front of him. *And to respect your elders, always lis-*

ten when they show or tell you something. Skye's eyes shifted from the Bluescale to what loomed ahead of them.

The doors.

We're almost there.

CLICK, CLACK, CLICK, CLACK. With each step he took, Skye felt anticipation bubbling up inside him. *Now's not the time to be emotional!* Skye thought as he suppressed his excitement. *I must be calm. The Bluescale guards are always calm.*

Skye continued to walk until the dragon in front of him came to a stop a few paces in front of the doors.

We're here.

"HALT! Who goes there?" Two guards leaped out from behind two stones, teeth bared and wings raised.

"There is no need for defensive measures, Zaffre and Strongclaw," the large dragon said.

The two guards immediately lowered their wings and stood straight. "Battlescar, sir," the male guard said.

"We are pleased to see you, sir," the female guard said.

"Thank you," Battlescar replied. "Today, I brought my student, Skye. This is the first day he will be guarding the Crystal."

"Understood. I presume that is he?" The male guard tilted a part of his wing at Skye.

"Yes, I am Skye, apprentice for guardianship of the Crystal," Skye said, feeling pride grow inside him.

"Ah, excellent! I am Strongclaw, one of the guards, and this is Zaffre, my partner," the male Bluescale guard said.

"We are honored to welcome you." Zaffre grinned.

"Now to business," Battlescar said. "Skye, follow me."

"Yes, sir."

Battlescar approached the stone doors, which were adorned with gemstones—dark-red garnets, bright-red rubies, and jet-black obsidian. Battlescar's dull, battle-worn talons tapped the gemstones.

Up, up, left, right, down, right, center. I believe that's the right pattern, Skye thought as he watched his teacher's talons. CLICK. Battlescar pushed on the stone doors, and they creaked open under his strength.

"Skye, follow me. You have one final test." With one more mighty push, the doors swung wide, and Battlescar stepped into the small cave. Skye followed closely, sky-blue eyes analyzing his new surroundings. The doors shut behind him with a THUD.

It was a small cave. The light-orange hue of the Glow-Crystals gave the cave light, and the cool stone made the room chilly. Skye, however, only cared about one thing in this small cave. He looked to the back and focused on the object he had spent his whole life training to protect.

The Dark Energy Crystal.

I've studied and seen so many gemstones in my life, Skye thought, *but this gemstone is unlike any I've seen in person.* Skye approached the gemstone, taking slow steps toward the black diamond. It sat upon a plain rock pedestal. Its edges were sharp as knives, and the surface was smooth and slick. Its black color was deeper and darker than any shard of obsidian he had handled.

It certainly is an impressive gemstone to look at, Skye thought, sitting back on his haunches. *This Crystal, however, is nothing short of horrible.* Skye's mind flashed back to screams, bloodshed, and battles, all the fault of this evil gemstone. He shook his head and clenched his jaw. *Now is not the time to recall such bloodshed. Now, I must be focused. Focused and proud.*

"Skye," Battlescar said, walking up beside Skye's left wing, "before you accept your new rank as my official guardian apprentice for the Dark Energy Crystal, I must do a final test of your knowledge. Are you ready?"

Skye looked up into Battlescar's dark-blue eyes. "I have been ready for this day all my life."

A sliver of a smile glimmered on Battlescar's serious face but quickly disappeared. "Very well. Where was the Dark Energy Crystal first discovered by dragons?"

"It was discovered in the Dragonback Ridge Mountains in central western Prodigus," Skye answered with a clear voice and his head held high.

"Correct. What is the main catastrophe that the Dark Energy Crystal caused?"

"The Dark Energy Crystal is at fault for the uprising of Demonheart and the Bloodclaws. Shortly after the uprising, they stole the Crystal and kept it with them for more than four hundred years."

"When was the Dark Energy Crystal retrieved from the Bloodclaws and put into safekeeping in the Bluescale cave?"

"It was retrieved from the Bloodclaws by the Bluescales in the Battle of the Crystal. While Bluescales attacked many Bloodclaws, the Dralerians, Emer and Iridigrarr, used their skills to retrieve the Dark Energy Crystal. However, Emer was the only Dralerian to live to see the victory of this battle." Skye sighed and turned his head to face the Dark Energy Crystal. "Many others died in the battle as well. I wonder, if the dragons who died were still alive today, what good they would do for us. If Iridigrarr were still alive, he'd be with Emer and the three new Chosen Ones. If Talonwing, Knifeclaw's old battle partner, were still here, Knifeclaw might smile and be happy at times. If Mother . . . if Mother . . ." Skye coughed and shook his head.

"It will be all right, Skye," Battlescar said, the slightest amount of sympathy sneaking into his voice. "Let us continue with the test. Why do we keep the Dark Energy Crystal hidden safe within the Bluescale cave?"

"The reason the Bluescales protect the Dark Energy Crystal within our Treasure Tunnels is because no matter what has been done to try to eliminate it, it has always reappeared, and it cannot be destroyed," Skye said. "Many dragon tribes have tried to destroy it with lava, fire, rocks, or ice, only to find it is indestructible. Some have tried to bury it underground, only to find that, days later, it has been dug up by thieves. Others have tried to utilize it for good purposes, but it has none, and it only brought misfortune upon those that tried to use it. That is why we Bluescales, the most trustworthy dragon tribe, protect it from the Bloodclaws, humans, and any lone dragon who tries to keep it. If any living creature with bad intentions gets possession of the Crystal, it could use it to destroy all other creatures and gain control of the world."

"Correct," Battlescar said. "There are two more questions. Should you ever bring any of your friends or the lower-ranked guards down into the Dark Energy Crystal Cave, and should you ever touch the Crystal?"

"You should never bring anyone lower than the rank of High Guard down into these tunnels and this cave. Only guards of High Rank and higher, as well as Vladmir, Knifeclaw, Majesty, Emer, and the Chosen Ones, are allowed down here. You must never touch the Dark Energy Crystal, because it turns anyone who touches it evil. Unless the creature touching it is wearing thick leather gloves or is already evil, anyone who touches the Crystal will immediately succumb to dark forces."

Skye looked up at Battlescar. "Did I pass?"

For the first time, Skye watched as the stern, frozen face of Battlescar lit up into a bright, beaming smile. His blue eyes filled with life. "You passed, young one."

Skye felt his heart beat rapidly; the happiness bubbled up again. *No! Repress the emotion!* "Thank you, Father—I mean Teacher!" Skye slapped his left foreclaw over his mouth. *I just broke the number-one rule! Always call your teacher "Sir" or "Teacher," even if he or she is your parent!*

To Skye's great surprise, Battlescar grinned and wrapped his right wing around him. "It is all right, son. You can be happy and proud of yourself in this moment." A calm silence filled the cave.

"I do wish Mother could have seen this," Skye whispered, leaning against the side of his father.

"I wish she could have seen this in person as well." Battlescar sighed. His mighty chest rumbled. "However, she's watching us from the Great Sky Above. She is proud of you. I am proud of you."

Skye's eyes widened, and he looked up at his father. *Did he just say he's proud of me?* Never, in Skye's whole life of training for this moment, had Battlescar ever said those words. He had only talked about ways Skye could improve.

But now he said he's proud of me. Skye tried to suppress his feelings, but he couldn't quite hold them in. A large grin spread across his face. "Thank you, Father. Thanks for all you've taught me. I'm so proud to be where I am today." He looked up at Battlescar. His father's big grin and gleaming eyes said it all.

Today has been such a good day, Skye thought. *Nothing can go wrong.*

"HISSSSS!"

"ROAR!"

"AAAAAAARGH!"

Skye's head whipped around to stare at the door. His eyes went wide as the sounds of smashing rocks, fighting, and scrabbling claws filled his ears.

"Father?"

"Skye, stay here." Battlescar's voice was cold. He lifted his wing off Skye and folded it against his body. He marched toward the door.

"Sir!" The doors opened with a creak. Strongclaw peeked into the room. There were small cuts along his scales. His eyes were wide with terror.

"What is the matter?" Battlescar demanded.

"There's a code red, Battlescar! Bloodclaws! Alert the —" His sentence was cut short as the jaws of a Bloodclaw snapped around his neck. Strongclaw's mouth hung open, and his eyes stared blankly at Skye. Blood gushed down the blue scales on his neck. The Bloodclaw tossed Strongclaw's limp neck aside and lunged forward. Its imposing black wings snapped open. CRACK! The doors broke off their hinges and crashed to the ground.

Oh, snake fangs, Skye thought, eyeing the Bloodclaw. It was larger than any of the ones he had read about. Blood was smeared on its talons and teeth. Its yellow eyes glowed in the dim light of the cave.

"Skye!" Battlescar's voice echoed in his head. *Oh, we're telecommunicating,* Skye thought. *So the Bloodclaws can't hear us.*

"Yes?" Skye telecommunicated back to his father.

"I'll fight against this Bloodclaw. You stand guard near the Dark Energy Crystal. If any other Bloodclaws come, fight. Understand?"

"Understood."

Skye watched as Battlescar lunged forward toward the Bloodclaw. He roared, a roar that echoed in the cave like thunder. His claws sliced through the Bloodclaw's scales. Blood dripped out of the wound.

"SCREEEEEECH!" the Bloodclaw cried.

Skye winced as it lunged at Battlescar. The two dragons became locked in a merciless battle.

Skye dashed over by the Dark Energy Crystal. He spread his wings and bared his teeth. *If any other Bloodclaw comes, it will have to get through me.* Skye paused. *I should telecommunicate for help.* Just as he was about to, a sleek Bloodclaw stalked through the doors. Its yellow eyes met Skye's.

"EEEEERARGH!" it roared, charging at Skye.

Skye growled and charged at the Bloodclaw. *Okay, Battle Technique 101: Aim for the stomach, head, neck, and wings. Fire is a great defense. Stay alive.* Skye beat his wings up in defense and blew out a stream of yellow-orange fire. The Bloodclaw's eyes went wide, and it leaned back.

It's working! Skye swiped his claw at the Bloodclaw and slashed its forearm. "YYYYYARRGH!" The Bloodclaw hissed and swiped at Skye's forearm. As the talons cut into Skye's scales, Skye winced, but he lunged forward and rammed the Bloodclaw in the chest with his horns. It wheezed and flew back into a wall. SLAM! The Bloodclaw crumpled to the ground.

Perfect! Skye thought as he ran forward. *Now, all I need to do is the Death Stab, and the enemy will be defeated!* Skye lifted his left forearm in the air above the dazed Bloodclaw, ready to strike—

SNAP! Piercing pain seared through Skye's left forearm. "AAAAARGH!" Skye screamed. He looked over. Another Bloodclaw had its jaws clenched around Skye's forearm. Skye shook his forearm. "Get off!" he yelled.

His eyes caught movement. The Bloodclaw he had slammed into the wall sat back on its haunches, lifting its claws into the air.

Oh, no, you don't. Skye opened his mouth. Fire streamed out and covered the Bloodclaw in flames. It collapsed to the ground.

Now, to take care of you, Skye thought as he glared at the Bloodclaw on his forearm. He winced as its teeth

dug deeper. Blood trickled down Skye's blue scales. Skye breathed out a burst of orange fire toward the Bloodclaw's feet. It leaped up, stamping its talons on the stone ground. Skye clawed the Bloodclaw's snout, drawing blood. The Bloodclaw growled, tightening its jaw around Skye's forearm. Skye's fear grew as he felt his bones snap and the sense of touch in his forearm disappear.

"GET OFF!" Skye yelled, furious. He smashed his right foreclaw onto the Bloodclaw's snout. Blood dripped out of its nose. The Bloodclaw's eyes turned to slits. It lifted its neck and head, still gripping Skye's forearm.

What is it doing? Skye thought, heart beating rapidly in his chest.

The Bloodclaw swung its head around. Skye flew in the air. He felt the joint in his left forearm SNAP. The Bloodclaw swung its head down. SLAM! Skye slammed against the ground. SNAP! His back snapped. His head hit the ground.

Ohh . . . Skye weakly opened his eyes. His vision was blurred. He tried to move. His body moved, but not fast enough.

"Er her her her," the Bloodclaw laughed. Skye's vision began to clear. The Bloodclaw had raised its right talon.

The Death Stab.

I can't move.

I'm going to die.

"Skye!"

What?

"Skye!" The deep voice grew louder. He could feel the heavy pounding of claws on the ground.

The Bloodclaw's claw began its descent.

"SKYE!"

A dragon lunged in front of Skye.

The Bloodclaw's claw slammed down into the dragon.

The dragon collapsed to the ground.

Fire streamed up from the blue dragon on the ground. The Bloodclaw dodged it and ran away to the Dark Energy Crystal.

No.

It picked up the Dark Energy Crystal in its jaws.

NO.

It dashed out of the cave.

NO!

Skye instinctively moved his left forearm to get up. His talon wouldn't move. Growling, he stumbled up with his right talon, wobbling on his feet.

That's when he saw the dragon who'd saved him.

"FATHER!"

Battlescar lay on the ground. His breathing was heavy. Blood gushed out of the gaping hole in his chest.

Skye tried to suppress his emotions. He tried. But the blood all over the ground, the missing Dark Energy Crystal, his forearm, and his father's wound were too much. Tears poured from his eyes.

"Father . . ." he choked out. He stumbled over next to his father. His left forearm dragged against the ground.

"Skye . . ." Battlescar gasped. His eyes opened just a crack as he struggled to breathe.

"I'm sorry. I failed."

"You . . . did your best. We both . . . did our best. These things . . . happen." Battlescar clenched his jaw and growled. "Th-this, final order: chase . . . the Bloodclaw. Kill it."

"But, Father, my forearm! Wait, final order?" The realization hit Skye like a rock. "No. NO! Stay here! Stay with us, you hear me! Stay! Don't leave!" Skye cried, stumbling forward and placing his talon on his father's left foreclaw. "I'm not leaving you!"

"Fulfill my order, Skye. You can do it, injury or not. The Dragon Spirit runs through you . . . the Greatwing will bless you with success. You can do it . . . Skye." His father's eyes opened again; they were filled with hope and sadness.

Skye grasped his father's foretalon. "I . . . I will fulfill . . . your order." He squeezed his eyes shut. Tears ran down his face as he let go of his father's foretalon. Skye limped away.

"I love you, son, and I'm proud of you . . . for all eternity."

Skye looked back at his father. "I love you, too."

His father smiled, and his eyes shut.

"Stay, Father! I'll be back!" Skye cried out. He stumbled out of the cave, breaking into an uneven run. He looked away from the torn corpses of Zaffre and Strongclaw. *I can't look at them.*

Skye kept running through the hallway, looking from side to side. *Where did that monster go?!* His mind screamed at him. *I need to find that Bloodclaw before my father . . .* Skye hissed and kept running. He searched.

His vision began to blur.

No! I must stay strong. I can find that Bloodclaw! Skye continued to look, but his left claw wobbled beneath him. Blood flowed down his broken forearm. His vision worsened, and he stumbled.

Finally, he collapsed.

No . . . I have to keep searching . . . I have to . . . Skye tried to keep his eyes open, but his eyelids drooped over his eyes.

I failed.

He descended into darkness.

CHAPTER 2

THE GEMSTONE WARRIORS

"The meeting of the Gemstone Warriors will come to order!"

Emer sat upon a large stone, her back talons strongly gripping the edge of the rock. CLICK CLICK CLICK. Emer rapped her green gemstone-encrusted tail against the rock; the noise resonated in the cave.

"Hey, I like this new cave," a young girl said, brushing a strand of blonde hair out of her face.

"I agree, Paris! We've never met in here before!" another girl said, her face illuminated by the lantern she carried.

"You're right, Gabby," a sapphire-blue Bluescale said, looking around the cave. "Emer, where did you get permission to use this for our meetings?"

"Well, Saphir, I talked with Majesty about our progress with our 'club,' as he calls it. He said that we're doing well and helping others in the cave, so he gave us our own room to meet in!" Emer spread out her foreclaws. "It's awesome,

I'll admit. It'll be large enough to train in once we clear out some of these rocks and add some GlowCrystals."

"Yes! He recognizes our greatness!" Paris cheered.

"What?" Emer said.

"We're the Chosen Ones, after all! All the Bluescales admire us! It's time Majesty realizes we need a room for our group!"

"I guess that's true," Emer said, scratching the scales behind her yellow ram-like horns, "but we should remember to stay humble. We must use our position as the Chosen Ones to help others."

"Okay, let's be honest here, how much helping can I do in a cave filled with dragons?" Paris asked, throwing her hands up in the air. "I'm still a supposed Dralerian stuck with only a human form, not an actual Dralerian that has a human form and can use a gemstone to transform into an epic dragon with awesome fire and fighting powers."

Oh no, not this discussion again, Emer thought, sighing. *Paris has been continually asking when she'll become an official Dralerian.*

"It has been quite a while since Vladmir said we'd get our powers," Gabby agreed. "Paris and I may be Chosen Ones and have this 'Dragon Spirit,' but we still only have this human form. You don't think he was lying, do you?" She looked at Paris with wide eyes.

"Vladmir never lies about those kinds of things," Emer said. "He gave all of you that riddle and found that Saphir was the one ready to gain his dragon form." *Saphir has adjusted quite well to it, actually*, Emer thought, eyeing

Saphir. *He can walk like a dragon now, and he can fight fairly well in dragon form.*

"That's mostly true," Saphir said.

"Wait, why did you say *mostly* true?" Paris asked, lowering her glasses and staring at Saphir. "You have a dragon form!"

"Yes, but I still can't breathe fire or use whatever element I have, and my telecommunication skills are horrible. I'm not the most useful Dralerian here, especially in the eyes of Knifeclaw." Saphir's wings drooped just the slightest bit.

Emer leaped down from her stone and landed with a THUD. She walked over to her friends. "Guys, it doesn't matter if we don't all have an element, or decent telecommunication skills, or even a dragon form yet! All that matters is that we help protect all of dragonkind! Paris and Gabby, Vladmir will give you your dragon forms when he knows that you're ready, okay? There's no need to worry." Emer looked at her friends with kind brown eyes.

"But it's been four weeks!" Paris exclaimed.

"The time will come, no matter how long it takes," Emer said. She faced Saphir. "And I'll work with you on your telecommunication skills. I'll admit, it's not an easy feat to talk with one another via your mind. Most of the lower- and middle-ranking dragons struggle with it. We'll find your element as well."

Emer looked at all her friends. "Remember, no matter how dark the times, we'll stick together."

"Because we're strong," Paris said.

"Because we're smart," Gabby said.

"Because we are the Chosen Ones from the Foretelling," Saphir said.

"Because we are friends to the end." Emer smiled at her friends. *I'm glad I have at least a few friends that appreciate me in both human and dragon form,* she thought. *That's not true of everybody.* The smile on her face disappeared. *Why do so many of the people I know want me to be somebody different from who I am?* she wondered, pulling her wings in closer to her body. *They want me to stop liking dragons. Start making other human friends. Become more interested in things I have no interest in. I want to just stay myself. My friends like me for who I am. The Bluescales like me for who I am. But what if change is necessary? Do I really have to change myself to fit into the human world? Who am I really supposed to be?* Emer sighed.

"Emer? Are you okay?" Saphir asked. There was worry in his green eyes.

She looked at him. *I don't want them to know I'm struggling. They have their issues. I must be strong for them.* "Yeah, I'm fine," Emer said with a smile. "Just thinking of how grateful I am to be here with the three of you."

"Oh," Saphir said, tilting his head. "Okay. That's good."

"Anyway, you called this Gemstone Warriors meeting because . . . ?" Paris asked, crossing her arms.

"I wanted to discuss the recent activities of the Bloodclaws," Emer said.

"But there haven't been any," Saphir stated. "At least, not according to the reports I've heard and read from the Bluescale scouts."

"Exactly." Emer nodded.

"You don't think they're plotting some other attack, do you?" Gabby fretted. "What if they've come up with some new way to attack us and steal the four of us and lock us in cages? I don't want that to happen again! I don't want to die!"

"Gabby, it's okay." Emer draped her right wing behind Gabby. "What Majesty wants us to do is come up with ways to protect ourselves and the other dragons here in the Bluescale cave so that can't happen again."

"Don't we already have a lot of defensive measures?" Paris asked.

"We can never have enough!" Gabby said. "You remember what happened four weeks ago! The Bloodclaws attacked our school! The Bloodclaws kidnapped us! Their leader, Demonheart, was ready to kill us! Then, when we thought we were safe, they flew after us and sneaked into the cave to try to kill us!"

"I agree with Gabby," Saphir said. "The more safety measures, the better. Although, I was thinking . . ."

"What?" Emer asked.

"We may have strategies to defeat the Bloodclaws and ways to protect ourselves and others, but what about ways to protect some of the valuables here in this cave? What about that Dark Crystal thing you told me about some time ago? Isn't that thing crucial to the Bluescales' safety?" Saphir asked.

"The what?" Paris asked.

"I think it's called the Dark Energy Crystal," Gabby said. "Didn't Majesty bring it up in one of his speeches?"

"Oh, the Dark Energy Crystal." Emer paused, putting her right foretalon on her chin. "I know there are guards who protect the Dark Energy Crystal day and night. However, it would be good to come up with a plan to protect it, in case a Bloodclaw did enter the cave to try to steal it."

"Can someone please explain to me what the Dark Energy Crystal is?" Paris demanded.

"The Dark Energy Crystal is a large, black, diamond-shaped crystal that can turn anyone who touches it evil," Emer explained.

"It makes things turn evil?" Gabby asked, eyes wide.

"Why do we keep it here, then?" Paris demanded. "Wouldn't it be easier to destroy it, or bury it in something? Ooh! We could cover it in concrete!"

"The reason we keep the Crystal here is because there's no way to get rid of it," Emer explained. "It's indestructible, so nothing can destroy it; even dropping it in a volcano wouldn't work. Whenever it's been buried, someone has always come to dig it out and take it for themselves. No matter what's been done, it always comes back. It's like a magnet that's attracted to dragons. The only option now is for a trustworthy dragon tribe, like the Bluescales, to guard it in a spot few know about. Only high-ranking Bluescales know where it's located."

"I still think concrete is the best option," Paris said.

"I don't think the dragons would accept that," Saphir stated. "They loathe any human creation, even something as simple as concrete. If we tried to bring it here, they would get rid of it immediately."

"Oh," Paris said. "Well, there went that idea."

"So, we have the Dark Energy Crystal?" Gabby asked. "I thought the Bloodclaws had it. Didn't Majesty say that in his speech?"

"We had it first, and then the Bloodclaws stole it from us when they rose to power," Emer said. "We stole it back a few years ago in the Battle of the Crystal. I was one of the dragons who actually sneaked into the cave to take it back from the Bloodclaws."

"But how did you touch it and bring it out of the cave if it turns everything evil?" Gabby asked.

"We wore gloves. If you wear thick, leather, steel-lined gloves when you handle it, its power doesn't hurt you."

"Who else went with you in the mission?" Paris asked. "I'd really like to meet them!"

Emer felt a twinge of sadness. *Iridigrarr, who died.* "Everyone else who went with me to take back the Dark Energy Crystal died at the talons of the Bloodclaws."

"Oh," Paris said quietly.

"Oh, I'm sorry," Gabby said, patting Emer's wing.

"It's fine." Emer sighed. "What happened has happened, and there's no changing the past. All we can do is look to the future."

"And to do that, we prepare," Saphir said, walking over and sitting next to Emer. "Emer, what would you think if we, the Gemstone Warriors, went to look at the Dark Energy Crystal to know what it looks like, where it's located, and how to protect it?"

"I'm not sure if the guards will let the three of you in," Emer said, looking at her friends, "but I know where it's located, and I know that I'm allowed to see it."

"You could actually show us the Dark Energy Crystal? Awesome!" Paris exclaimed, jumping in the air.

"Well," Emer said, a sly smile on her face, "we must decide in a fair and honest way as a team. All in favor of seeing the Dark Energy Crystal and its location for educational and protective purposes, say aye." Emer raised her right forearm.

"Aye," Gabby said, raising her right arm.

"Aye," Saphir said, raising his right forearm.

"Oh yeah, aye!" Paris exclaimed.

"It's settled, then," Emer said. "We will all go to see the Dark Energy Crystal so we can come up with a strategy for us, the Gemstone Warriors, to protect it. I can personally guarantee that none of you will have ever seen anything like it in your life."

* * * * *

That was my most interesting experience in the Flight Tunnels yet, Emer thought. She and her friends were walking side by side in dim, wide tunnels. *Those Flight Tunnels are always busy, no matter the time of day. Poor Saphir. He's only flown in open space, and then to be stuck in a narrow tunnel with dragons flying everywhere, not to mention a human on your back . . .* Emer sighed. *I'll practice more with him later.*

"Those tunnels were so cool!" Paris said. "What are they called again?"

"Those are Flight Tunnels. They're kind of like elevators or staircases, only for dragons," Emer explained. "They help us get to where we need to go."

"Fascinating," Gabby said. "That's a cool thing the dragons came up with. It makes everything efficient and easy for all the Bluescales."

"Only if you're used to tight spaces and angry dragons." Saphir sighed. "Why did that one dragon call me a 'bat-winged barebelly,' anyway?"

"Because just like humans, some dragons have loose tongues and no respect," Emer grumbled. "They don't think before they call names. Okay, I just want to say one thing beforehand—no touching the Dark Energy Crystal. Stay at least ten paces away from it. If the guards say we can't look at it, we will turn around without a fuss, and we must stay quiet and—get down!" Emer hissed, flaring her wings and shoving her friends behind a large rock in the hallway.

"What the—" Paris said.

"What are you doing?" Gabby asked.

"What—OH," Saphir said, looking at the sight before him. He ducked behind the rock.

Emer pointed her right foretalon. Paris and Gabby gasped.

Inactivity for four weeks, Emer thought, the voice in her head snarling. *That's over now.*

A Bloodclaw, smeared with red stains and burns, towered over the body of a sky-blue Bluescale. The body lay in a pool of its own blood.

CHAPTER 3

THE BLOODCLAWS ATTACK

For four weeks, there's been no activity. None at all.

That has all changed now.

Saphir was hiding behind the stone with his friends. He eyed the Bloodclaw, green eyes wide with fear.

"How did this thing get in?" Saphir asked. "I thought we blocked off all the entrances from previous attacks!"

"We did!" Emer hissed. "It must have crept in through the Mining Tunnels!"

"Mining Tunnels?" Gabby asked.

"Shh! I'll explain later," Emer said. "I need to telecommunicate for help." She stared off into space.

I can't wait for the day I'm better at telecommunication, Saphir thought. *And have an element. That will be nice. Then Knifeclaw will stop putting so much pressure on me.*

"Guys, it's getting really close to that Bluescale," Paris said, looking up at Saphir and Emer. "We need to stop it."

"We have to wait," Saphir whispered, watching the Bloodclaw. "Let Emer come up with a plan."

"But the Bluescale will die!"

"If he's still alive."

"Or he'll be eaten in front of us!"

"They're cannibals?!" Gabby said, eyes wide with horror.

"Augh! I don't know! We just need to do something!" Paris said, picking up a rock.

"Paris, you'd better not do what I think you might do," Saphir said. *She can't go out there. Not without a plan!*

"Well, you guys didn't come up with a plan. So I came up with one." Paris stepped out into the open. "HEY, UGLY! EAT ROCK!" She hurled the rock at the Bloodclaw. BONK! It hit the Bloodclaw's snout. Blood trickled out of one nostril.

"HISSSSSSS!" The Bloodclaw's eyes narrowed. Its shiny black talons clicked the ground as the monster came toward the rock they were hiding behind.

"Okay, Paris, what's the next part of the plan?" Saphir asked, heart beating rapidly in his chest.

"What next part? That was my plan!" Paris said.

"That was your plan?!" Saphir hissed.

"Oh, great," Gabby whispered.

"What is going on?" Emer demanded, head whipping toward them. "I try to telecommunicate for help and—" She glanced at the Bloodclaw. "Everyone get down!"

Saphir ducked his head. Orange fire swept around the sides of the rock.

"Okay, here's the plan: Saphir, you and I will distract the Bloodclaw and try to get rid of it. Gabby, Paris, go hide behind the hurt Bluescale and see if you can tend to it in any way. Got it?" Emer said.

"Got it," they all said.

"Good." The fire that had been blasting around the rock died down. "Let's go now!" Emer sprang out into the open. Paris and Gabby followed, running beside Emer.

Saphir leaped out in the open and charged at the Bloodclaw.

"HISSSSS!" The Bloodclaw swept its talons at Saphir. Saphir ducked out of the way and slammed his horns into the Bloodclaw's side. The red dragon tumbled back. As Saphir glanced around, he saw something hidden in the corner.

"Emer," he called out and pointed to the odd rock he saw. "Is that . . . ?"

"The Dark Energy Crystal," Emer said, eyes wide. "Saphir, guard the Crystal. I'll defeat this Bloodclaw." She tapped the emerald on her chest. The scales on her claws became a shimmery emerald green.

Ah, the emerald talons, Saphir thought. *Now that she's sharpened the scales and talons on her claws to make them more resistant, hopefully this fight will end fast.*

Emer lunged at the Bloodclaw. She swiped her right talon across its face. It hissed, blood dripping down its red scales.

Saphir ran over beside the Dark Energy Crystal, claws trembling as he stopped beside it. *The Crystal . . . if I touch it, I'm done for. I must be careful.* He spread his wings slowly, glancing at the Dark Energy Crystal, then back at the fight. *I must be prepared to attack.*

He watched the fight with alert eyes. Emer swiped her talons at the Bloodclaw, but the Bloodclaw dodged all attacks. It leaped forward, talons outstretched. Emer dodged and sliced her talons across its underbelly.

"SCREEEEEECH!" The Bloodclaw howled and breathed out a torrent of flame. Emer sidestepped the attack and lunged forward, right talon raised in the air for the Death Stab. She aimed right for its chest.

The Bloodclaw dodged, but not enough. Emer's talon plunged into the Bloodclaw's side. Saphir cringed and shut his eyes.

"EEEEYARGH!" the Bloodclaw cried out. Blood gushed from the wound. It stumbled and fell toward the ground, but caught itself and stood up.

Oh no, Saphir thought. *The Death Stab will only end a fight if the hit is directly to the chest. Emer hit the Bloodclaw's side. This is not good . . .*

The Bloodclaw's yellow eyes focused on Emer. It lunged forward. Emer dodged, but the Bloodclaw's sharp tail swung up and tripped Emer, its spines cutting her legs.

Emer growled as she hit the ground. She started to get up, but the Bloodclaw breathed out a gust of fire. Emer rolled to the side. The Bloodclaw dashed away from Emer . . . straight toward Saphir.

"Saphir! This is simple battle technique! You've got this!" Emer yelled, claws scrabbling against the ground.

Simple battle technique, Saphir told himself. *Yeah, telling myself that is not going to calm me down.* He stared into the yellow eyes of the Bloodclaw. It leaped in the air.

Saphir swept his talon across its underbelly. The Bloodclaw tumbled to the side, wheezing as blood dripped out of the new wound.

"HISSSS!" Fire blasted out of its mouth. Saphir dodged and leaped to the side.

WHACK! Saphir found himself falling to the ground. Sharp pain seared through his forearms and back legs. *I must get up! I have to stop that Bloodclaw!*

The Bloodclaw leaped over his head. Saphir's eyes widened and his heart sank as he watched the Bloodclaw.

It had the Dark Energy Crystal in its jaws.

"NO!" Emer yelled, leaping at the Bloodclaw. She breathed a plume of bright-green fire at the monster. The Bloodclaw evaded her attack and ran into a nearby dark, narrow tunnel.

"No!" Saphir yelled, getting up and running toward the tunnel.

"I'll help you get it back!" Emer exclaimed, running beside Saphir.

A whoosh of fire and a mighty roar caught Saphir's attention. He turned and faced the entryway for the wide tunnels.

Majesty, Saphir thought, heart sinking in his chest. Saphir eyed the majestic leader of the Bluescales, whose midnight-blue scales and golden horns gleamed in the dim light from the GlowCrystals. His eyes, however, were cold and dark. *What will he say when we tell him the news?*

"Emer," Majesty said, voice echoing in the tunnels. "You telecommunicated to me about an attack?"

"Yes, sir," Emer said, looking at the small tunnel, then

turning to face Majesty. "The Bloodclaw ran down that tunnel. We were about to go after it."

"Guards!" Majesty thundered. Ten Bluescales clad in armor marched up beside him. "Go down into the Mining Tunnels. Find the Bloodclaw. Exterminate it immediately!"

They nodded, dashing past Majesty, Emer, and Saphir, running into the dark, narrow tunnel.

"That Bloodclaw will be taken care of," Majesty said, looking from the Mining Tunnel entrance to Emer. "Are there any dragons injured?"

"We came down here and found this poor dragon." She pointed at the sky-blue dragon as Gabby and Paris approached Emer.

"Have you found any more injured?"

"No, sir. We had to deal with the Bloodclaw."

"Hopefully, it was taken care of successfully," a voice snarled. Saphir looked toward the tunnel's entryway. A dull-blue dragon with cracked horns and a scar over his eye stalked into the cave. *Knifeclaw*, Saphir thought. *All hope of sympathy is gone now.*

"Sir, it was a Rank 3 Bloodclaw. It was hard to battle," Emer said, looking at Knifeclaw.

"That should not be an excuse for the Chosen Ones, especially two dragon-form Dralerians," Knifeclaw growled.

"It escaped us both," Saphir admitted. *I don't want Emer to get blamed for all this.*

"Well, I'm not surprised. This Dralerian is useless without an element, anyway," Knifeclaw said, flicking his tail at Saphir.

"It was not his fault!" Emer said, flaring her wings. "He is still learning!"

"ENOUGH!" Majesty thundered, wings flaring. "Arguing over a Bloodclaw escape will get us nowhere!"

"Then we should go find it and kill it!" Knifeclaw argued, baring his teeth. "It's useless to stand here!"

Majesty glared at Knifeclaw. "Knifeclaw, I sent down our ten most skilled guards. They will find the Bloodclaw and eliminate it. Emer and Saphir must remain present here because they are witnesses." He stared down at Emer and Saphir. "What about the Dark Energy Crystal? Is it safe? Did the Bloodclaw take any other valuables?"

Emer froze. Saphir watched as she shuffled her wings and looked at the ground. "There was one valuable taken," Emer muttered.

"What was it?" Majesty demanded. "A diamond? A pearl? A GlowCrystal?"

Emer looked up at them, then at the ground. *She's worried*, Saphir thought, frowning. *She knows they'll be disappointed and furious beyond words.*

"Speak up, Emer. We do not have all day to frolic in these tunnels," Knifeclaw said.

"It was the Dark Energy Crystal." Saphir let the words tumble out of his mouth.

Majesty and Knifeclaw went still. Emer looked up at Saphir. The tunnels fell silent.

Saphir trembled as the eyes of the two most important and powerful Bluescales stared straight into his soul.

"We did our best," Saphir said, "but it's gone."

CHAPTER 4

ALL WE HAVE LOST

I hope that he makes it.

Emer sat, leaning against the cool wall of a cave. Gabby was sitting next to her; Paris was pacing around the room; Saphir was wrapping bandages around his forearms. Emer's eyes slowly scanned her familiar surroundings: GlowCrystals with many different colors, herbs hung up to dry, a copper pot in the corner, and shelves containing vast quantities of the medicinal knowledge of dragons.

Vladmir's cave is normally a place of comfort for me, Emer thought, *but today it's a place of waiting and sorrow.* She fingered the bandages around her forearms. Her mind was still whirling about the earlier events.

Three Bluescales dead, two Bloodclaws dead, Emer thought with a grimace. *How did no one know about this attack? Did the Bloodclaws attack so quickly the Bluescales had no time to telecommunicate? Or was everyone down there that inexperienced with telecommunication? It doesn't make any sense.*

Ugh, it's not as if I'm not dealing with enough already, Emer thought, a burst of smoke poofing out of her nose. *Most of the kids in school won't accept me for who I am. They follow Lucy's lead in taunting me. My mom has been trying to get me to draw less and interact with people more, especially Lucy's clique. She just doesn't understand how horrible Lucy really is! Besides, I'm purposely trying to avoid Lucy. I can never let her discover my secret! And now I'm dealing with a Bloodclaw attack and multiple Bluescale deaths? Are the Celestials and the Greatwing out to get me?*

"How do you think that dragon we saved is doing?" Gabby asked, looking toward a nearby door.

"I don't know." Emer sighed. "I hope he makes it. I hope at least one dragon survives this horrid event."

"I agree," Saphir said. "The Dark Energy Crystal slipped out of our talons. Majesty and Knifeclaw were angrier and more disappointed in us than words can say, and when we tried to heal that dragon with our gemstones, it didn't work!"

"That was weird," Emer said. "It worked for us back when we got hurt, so why not him?"

"You know, if I had my dragon form, I could have helped a lot," Paris said. "Maybe then we would have defeated that Bloodclaw."

"You didn't listen to me and went out in the open to throw a rock at the Bloodclaw!" Saphir said.

"An extra dragon or Dralerian in dragon form may have helped us, but we didn't have one, so now we face the consequences," Emer said. "I still can't believe one of the dragons that died was Battlescar himself. He was a superior warrior."

"Who was he?" Gabby asked.

"He was a dragon who fought in the Battle of the Crystal. He defeated many Bloodclaws. Because of this, he gained a place in the Council and was decreed head guardian of the Dark Energy Crystal. I can't believe I didn't recognize his son, either."

"Wait, that sky-blue dragon was his son?" Paris asked.

"Yes. Skye. Younger brother to Stonehorn, in fact," Emer said. "Stonehorn will be devastated to hear about this." She looked at the ceiling. Her stomach twisted inside her. *Will I ever become immune, so that every time I see some wretched sight my heart and mind won't descend into sadness?*

"We've all done the best we can to help Skye and fix this situation," Gabby said. "Now, we just need to wait and make sure he pulls through. I think he'll turn out all right."

Emer looked at Gabby. *She's gotten much wiser since getting those private lessons from Vladmir.*

SLAM! The door to Vladmir's cave swung open with violent ferocity. A pale-blue Bluescale charged into the room, his eyes wide with panic. He dashed over to Emer and grabbed her shoulders.

"WHERE'S MY BROTHER? HOW IS HE? HOW DID THIS HAPPEN?" he yelled as tears ran down his face.

"Stonehorn, you have to be a little quieter," Emer said. "They're doing surgery on him right now. Giving him stitches, bandages, everything he needs."

"What if they don't use the right stitch method? What if he gets a horrible infection? What if he DIES?" Stonehorn cried out. He let go of Emer's shoulders and slouched back on his haunches, his head drooping.

"Stonehorn, we've done all we can do," Saphir said.

"All we can do is wait," Gabby said, walking over and patting his foreclaw.

"Wait, what about the others?" Stonehorn asked. "I heard there were other guards. Was Battlescar, my father, there? Is he alive or dead?"

Emer paused, trying to think of what to say. "I . . . I . . . ." She hesitated, then closed her mouth.

Stonehorn shook his head, tears dripping. "You know what, you don't even have to tell me. I know." He walked over to a nearby stone wall and pounded it with his right foretalon. "If . . . if he's truly dead . . . after the argument we had . . . I'll never be able to forgive myself," he mumbled. Emer barely heard it, but she heard enough.

Memories of arguing with her mom flashed into Emer's mind. *So Stonehorn has had issues with a parent as well,* Emer thought. *I know how he feels. I should go comfort him.* She shook her tail, preparing to get up.

CREAK. The set of doors by Emer swung open. She looked toward them. The gleaming white scales on the approaching Bluescale reassured Emer the answers were on their way. All heads turned to face him.

"Vladmir, how is he?" Emer asked.

"Is he alive?" Stonehorn asked, head jerking to face Vladmir. Emer could see worry, fear, and grief in Stonehorn's eyes.

"He made it through the surgery," Vladmir declared. "He is in recovery now."

Emer breathed out a sigh. *Out of all the deaths, the Gemstone Warriors only managed to save one dragon.*

"Can I go see him?" Stonehorn quickly asked.

"Unfortunately, no. He must have solitude to recover faster, at least for tonight," Vladmir said. "However, if you want to visit him tomorrow, you are welcome."

"I'll wait here so I can see him right away," Stonehorn declared.

"Thank you so much, Vladmir." Emer walked up to him. "I'm so grateful for all you've done." She sighed, then looked at the ground.

"Emer, I know this is hard," Vladmir said. "But it is not your whole fault. You and your friends were merely witnesses to what had taken place. You did all you could."

"Tell that to Knifeclaw and Majesty," Paris said. "They scolded us for not stopping this whole catastrophe."

"Yeah. Knifeclaw even made sure that Emer and I would get less food tonight in the meal cave," Saphir added.

Vladmir growled. "Shame on them. Our two leaders should know better," he muttered to himself. "I will talk with Majesty and Knifeclaw tonight. They should know that it truly is the guards' fault for not stopping the Bloodclaw."

"But we were down there when it was still alive! We should have been able to kill it!" Emer exclaimed.

"And yet the high-ranked guards could not," Vladmir said, "and they have had many more years of battle training than the four of you have had combined."

Emer opened her mouth, but she found she had nothing to counter his remark.

"If fully grown adult dragons cannot stop a powerful Bloodclaw, how could four young Dralerians stop it?"

"But isn't that what we're for?" Gabby asked. "We're the Chosen Ones. We're supposed to be able to stop anyone and save everything."

"You did save one. You saved the life of the Bluescale, Skye," Vladmir said, a tired smile on his face. "Do not worry about the comments from Majesty and Knifeclaw. A horrible event has just taken place, and they tried to sort out what took place by blaming the four of you. I will talk to them about this incident. But for now, I want all of you to go and rest. The High Ranks will take care of everything else."

"Thanks," Emer said, smiling. She turned away and headed for the door, motioning her friends to follow.

"Good night, Vladmir," Emer said.

"Good night, Emer," Vladmir returned.

Emer pushed open the door, letting her friends exit first. As Emer walked out the doors, she heard Vladmir shuffle some papers.

"Poor Skye. It's a pity that some dragons must lose in order to live," he said.

Before Emer could question what that meant, the doors shut with a CREAK. Emer was left to ponder.

* * * * *

Everything was black. Everything had been black.

Until now.

Cracks of light peeked in through the darkness.

What . . . what is that light? Skye thought. He felt his groggy mind awaken as his eyes opened slowly. A purple light surrounded him, and there were stone walls all around him. He lay on a pile of soft buffalo hides.

Where am I? What happened? He searched his mind. He couldn't remember.

Then it hit him.

The importance of the day, the love his father had shown, the Bloodclaws, the Dark Energy Crystal, the deaths of high-ranking guards Zaffre and Strongclaw, and his father's one final command: "Kill the Bloodclaw."

Kill the Bloodclaw for Battlescar! For my dying father! he thought, baring his teeth. He tried to stand up. Pain streaked through his body, and he collapsed to the ground in shock.

What happened? What is going on? He tried to stand up again. The pain attacked him again. He collapsed onto the hides once more.

Was I hurt this badly? Why am I in so much pain? He tried to lift his left foreclaw to scratch his head. It did not reach.

What? He tried again.

What is wrong with my—

Skye's confused mind yelled but then stopped. He stared at his left forearm in disbelief.

His upper forearm was bandaged heavily with white bandages; there were tints of red and yellow in the fabric bandaging. But his lower forearm, his strong, good lower forearm . . .

It was gone.

Skye couldn't hold back his emotions anymore. He collapsed in his bedding and cried.

CHAPTER 5

IRIDIGRARR'S PLAN

CLICK. CLACK. CLICK. CLACK.

Iridigrarr paced in his cave, golden-yellow talons sliding across the cool stone beneath. *I put my plan into action long ago,* he thought. *Why hasn't at least one of the Bloodclaws returned? My plan has to have worked. I must prove my value to Demonheart.*

I have to prove to him I'm strong. Because I am stronger than he is. Smarter than he is.

Smarter than he will ever be.

CREAK. The door moved. Iridigrarr turned his head, red eyes glaring at the door.

"Unless you have something useful for me, leave."

A Bloodclaw limped through the doorway. Iridigrarr flexed his foreclaws and turned around, preparing to tackle the Bloodclaw. He froze.

It held the Dark Energy Crystal in its jaw.

My plan worked.

"Put the Dark Energy Crystal over on that pedestal, behind that rock," Iridigrarr demanded. The Bloodclaw looked at him, then behind the rock. It limped over and tilted its head sideways, placing the Crystal onto the pedestal. It backed away. Iridigrarr eyed its teeth and talons. *Bloodstains,* he thought. *No survivors remain, or will remain. Good.*

"Ackurr . . . nar erer?" it wheezed. Iridigrarr noticed all the wounds it had. *Cuts, burns . . . someone even tried a Death Stab on this dragon.* Iridigrarr pondered what to do with this useless Bloodclaw.

"Your reward is eternal peace," Iridigrarr snarled, swiping his right foreclaw across the Bloodclaw's throat. It collapsed to the ground without a sound.

Iridigrarr growled. *Now I have a disgusting corpse in my cave. I'll dispose of it later.*

CREAK. The door opened again.

"Oh, what in the name of the Greatwing—" Iridigrarr snarled as he looked at the door. He stopped.

A large, imposing Bloodclaw stood in the doorway. His scales were blood-red; his talons were obsidian-black, and large, silver spines ran down his back. Iridigrarr stared into the Bloodclaw's eyes, a deep yellow, surrounded by black marks, like Iridigrarr's own eye marks.

Demonheart.

"Well, well, well," Demonheart said. "So tell me, did your pathetic plan actually work?"

"Of course it worked. It wasn't planned by you," Iridigrarr snapped.

Demonheart glared at Iridigrarr, and smoke billowed up out of his long, red snout. "Do not insult me, weakling," Demonheart hissed. "I could defeat you with two swipes of my claws." Demonheart stared at the corpse on the ground. "If you anger me, I'll make you look like that."

"I could fight back," Iridigrarr threatened.

"HA HA HA HA! With what? Your weak fire?" Demonheart chuckled. "Pathetic!" he sneered. "I could easily defeat you."

Iridigrarr glared at a nearby rock. He couldn't make eye contact with Demonheart now, not with all the dark thoughts in his mind.

"What's most pathetic is that you have a gemstone." Demonheart snickered, pointing at the red garnet on Iridigrarr's chest. "Yet you can't seem to release your power! I've waited patiently, but no sign. No human form, no glorious fire powers. You really are useless, battle-wise!"

"I am still smart. I got back the Dark Energy Crystal." Iridigrarr bared his teeth. *How dare he insult me in such a manner*, he hissed in his mind.

"Where is it, then? Ah, how I have missed it!" Demonheart sighed, looking around.

"It is around this rock," Iridigrarr answered. He walked around to look at the Dark Energy Crystal. He could hear Demonheart following him.

"I cannot wait to put it back in my—WHAT IS IT SITTING ON?" Demonheart's voice roared.

Iridigrarr looked at the Dark Energy Crystal's pedestal. *The pedestal I carved*, Iridigrarr thought with a smirk. He eyed every curve, every detailed dragon carved into the side of the stone. *I seem to be an artist at heart.* "This pedestal is something I created so the Dark Energy Crystal would have something majestic to sit on, something worthy of its greatness."

"This is worthless! You heard my orders well and clear that this Crystal would stay in my cave! Destroy the pedestal at once!" Demonheart ordered.

"I must say no," Iridigrarr said.

"WHAT?" Demonheart roared. "How dare you disobey me!" His foreclaws smashed into a nearby stalagmite, turning it to pebbles.

"I am only doing so for the Dark Energy Crystal's safety," Iridigrarr said. "One of the lower-ranking Bloodclaws could get its grimy talons onto the Crystal and ruin it, maybe even break it."

"The Dark Energy Crystal cannot break!" Demonheart scoffed. "It was with me for four hundred years, and there's not a crack on its surface!"

"But a fellow Bloodclaw could steal it. You know how they are. And they all expect to find it in your cave. None of them will think to look for it here."

Demonheart was silent. Iridigrarr knew he was getting somewhere. *I have to get my way*, Iridigrarr thought. *I must keep the Crystal for my own uses.*

"True," Demonheart said. He growled a long, agonizing growl, gripping his head with his right foretalon. "I suppose . . . you are . . . right," he choked out.

Iridigrarr smirked a tiny, evil smile.

"It must only be used for the plan," Demonheart demanded. "Understood?"

"Yes, as bait," Iridigrarr said, rolling his eyes. "I will use it to lure Emer here, so I can rip out her emerald."

"Ah, yes." Demonheart laughed. "I cannot wait for that moment to come!"

"It will come sooner if you let me outside of this cave," Iridigrarr stated.

Demonheart growled. "You are not allowed to leave this cave, and you know it! Understood?"

The creaking of a hatch, the shutting of a small, wooden door, and the flutter of coal-black wings interrupted Demonheart. Iridigrarr held out his right foreclaw. A shiny black crow fluttered onto his golden-yellow talons. Its golden collar and red gemstone glinted in the light from the torches on the walls.

"What," Demonheart spat, "is that?"

"This is my spy," Iridigrarr said with a clever grin.

"How is he your spy? He's a crow!"

"He just is." Iridigrarr shrugged.

"Hmph," Demonheart growled, walking toward the door. "Spend more time planning and less time goofing off with stupid birds." Demonheart opened the door, then paused. "By the way, I just thought of a way you could leave the cave and become my official assistant."

"How?"

"Breathe fire!" Demonheart yelled. "You'll never be out of here as long as you only breathe sparks!" Demonheart yanked the door shut behind him. SLAM!

Iridigrarr stood still. Then he roared. He smashed his talons into a nearby stalagmite. He tried breathing fire, but only sparks came out. He collapsed. The frightened crow flew around and landed on a nearby rock.

"I can't breathe fire!" Iridigrarr yelled. He closed his eyes, head hanging. *I don't know why*, he thought. *I can feel my fire sac in my throat. I feel as if I once had fire. I feel as if I could once even telecommunicate. I feel as if I once had power, but now it's gone! If only . . .*

His eyes opened.

He stood up and walked over to the Dark Energy Crystal. Part of his mind had no idea what he was doing, but his subconscious knew exactly what to do. *Oh, Demonheart, you can't tell when a dragon is lying, can you?* he thought, facing the Dark Energy Crystal. *I'm planning on doing much more with this Crystal than you think. I'm sure I can find ways to use the Dark Energy Crystal for my own needs.*

I'm sure I can harness its power for myself.

He placed his foreclaw on the Dark Energy Crystal. Red lightning sizzled on its smooth surface, channeling up Iridigrarr's right forearm. He winced in pain but kept his hand on the Dark Energy Crystal.

"Give me back my powerful fire," he snarled. "And give me a disguise."

Red lightning flew from the Dark Energy Crystal and covered Iridigrarr's body. Iridigrarr winced in pain. The lightning yanked at his red scales and yellow chest plates. He was in agony. *But it will be worth it!*

The lightning stopped.

The crow cawed and flapped its wings.

Iridigrarr opened his eyes. He looked at his foreclaws. His talons and scales were the color of coal, his talons as black as obsidian. He dashed over to a shard of glass hanging on his wall. He gawked, then grinned, at his reflection. His chest plates were obsidian-black, and the undersides of his wings were as black as the night sky. The ram-like horns on his head and the spikes, trailing from his head to his tail, were a shiny black as well. His sclera was pitch-black, and the garnets on his chest and tail were jet-black.

Iridigrarr chuckled. Then he laughed. He laughed an evil laugh that shook the stalagmites in his cave.

"I look just like a shard of obsidian." He laughed again, then paused. "Obsidian. Obsidian will be my pseudonym."

"CAW! CAW!" the crow squawked, bobbing its head.

"How did I do it?" Iridigrarr said, staring at the crow. "I'm . . . not fully sure. It's just whispers of ideas that appear in my subconscious mind sometimes." Suddenly, pain bolted through his right forearm. He hissed and grabbed it with his other claw.

It's acting up again, Iridigrarr thought, staring at the long scar on his right forearm. *That scar . . . I have no idea where it came from, but it always hurts after I get my subconscious ideas.*

"CAW, CAW!"

"Oh, don't worry. I'm all right," Iridigrarr said, shaking the pain out of his right forearm, then holding out his claw. The crow flew over and perched on his talon. "Hold still," Iridigrarr murmured, fingering the red gemstone on its collar, unclipping the pendant with a CLICK. He tapped the gemstone three times, then set it down.

A holographic image of the sky showed up, followed by an image of a large building.

I may not have fire, but I can still breathe sparks, Iridigrarr thought. *I had just enough fire within me to weld a garnet and ruby together and create a gemstone that can scan and record its surroundings. This will help me find Emer in her weakest form.*

Her human form.

"What is this place?" he asked the crow. "A tutoring place for young humans? A . . . what's it called? A school?"

"CAW!"

"Are you sure this is the right place?"

"CAW, CAW!"

"Emer's human form is there? You saw the Bloodclaws attack here when they captured her friends?"

"CAW! CAW, CAW, CAW!"

"I'm not planning to send other Bloodclaws to destroy them!" Iridigrarr snapped. "This time I'm going to be discreet, finding Emer and the rest of them in their human forms and learning everything about them, from their strengths to their weaknesses."

"CAW!"

"I can't kill them on sight," Iridigrarr said, rolling his eyes. "Too many humans would take notice. Besides, all the threats of killing are just to please our stupid overlord, Demonheart. It would be much more useful to get her and the other cursed Chosen Ones to bow down to me. To use their mighty powers for me. Even if I have to push them to the brink of death to get them to join me, I will do it. But, if

I do manage to find them in their human forms, how can I get them to trust me and fall into my talons?"

Iridigrarr slowly looked around his cave, from the black gemstone on his chest to the Dark Energy Crystal in the corner.

"Perfect." Iridigrarr grinned, his teeth glinting in the torch-light. "I have a plan. A plan so detailed, so dastardly, Demon-heart's feeble mind would never be able to figure it out."

"CAW, CAW!" The crow flapped its wings, ebony eyes shining.

"Oh, Demonheart's plan? I'll use it to cover up my new plan. His plan deals with death and revenge, all the typical stuff. But my new plan, my useful plan, will have the Chosen Ones cowering at my claws. Emer will be in disbelief." He looked at his crow. "She'll never see me coming."

CHAPTER 6

CHANGE

Emer soared through the calm night air. The breeze gently blew beneath her wings, and the stars shone in the dark sky. She scanned the ground, looking at house after house.

Come on, I hate it when I lose sight of where my house is, Emer thought. *At least I got Gabby, Paris, and Saphir, who's now in his human form as Raider, home safely.* Her eyes focused on a specific house.

There it is! Emer dove down toward the house. She knew no one was awake at this hour. She hovered above her small backyard and placed her right foretalon on her emerald. There was a flash of light. Emer felt herself grow smaller. Her scales disappeared, her horns were replaced by long, brown hair, her wings and tail shrank and disappeared from sight, and her T-shirt and jeans morphed back onto her.

She was once again Bella, a thirteen-year-old girl.

She dropped to the ground and landed on her feet. She adjusted her pink glasses and stared into her small house. *I guess Mom isn't home yet,* Bella thought as she unlocked and opened the sliding door. *She has some long shifts at the hospital. I guess that's bittersweet, because it allows me to make trips to the Bluescale cave.* She clicked on some lights and dashed up the stairs. The carpet felt rough on her feet as she approached her room and entered.

She walked slowly into her small room, faced her bed, and collapsed onto it. The soft warmth of the bed comforted her. *Unfortunately, I can't go to bed yet.* She sat up and walked toward her desk, pulling out a textbook. *It's not like I could fall asleep peacefully now, not after all the events from tonight.*

So she read. She studied. She wrote. Book after book, paper after paper, she diligently worked. Finally, when all her homework was complete, she pulled out a piece of paper and drew. Dragons danced across the paper on which she sketched. All the while, however, her mind was plagued with Bloodclaws, dying Bluescales, fighting, injuries, and death. *I wish these thoughts would go away.*

The sound of the door and the jingle of keys caught Bella's attention. She glanced at the clock. *One o'clock. She's been later than that before, I suppose.* She listened as the stairs creaked. The noise grew closer.

"Bella? Are you in here?" a voice asked. The door creaked open. Bella turned to face her mother. Her blue eyes looked straight at Bella. She brushed a strand of reddish-blonde hair out of her face. She was still wearing her scrubs, and her eyes looked worn and tired.

"Hi, Mom."

"You're up late. Is your homework done?"

"Yep." Bella gestured to the large pile of textbooks on her desk.

"That's good."

"Oh, Mom! Want to see this cool drawing of dragons I—"

"Did you go to the school dance tonight?"

Bella's heart sank. *I thought she'd forgotten about that,* Bella thought. Her mind flashed back to last year's school dance. Too much noise, too many people, too many flashing lights, too much of everything that overwhelmed her. *Too much social media, too,* Bella thought with a shudder. *Too many people who could catch me transforming from dragon to human or back again and post it, revealing everything about me to the world.*

"I didn't go," Bella admitted.

Her mom frowned. "Why not? You know it'd be a great way for you to get out of the house."

"Well, maybe," Bella said. "I hung out with my friends instead. Here, you should look at this drawing—"

"Couldn't you have brought your friends to the party?"

"Maybe, I don't know! Can you look at—"

"Hold on a second," Bella's mom said. "You should have gone to the school dance. You could have brought your friends with you and had a great time, and you could have met more people and had fun like a normal girl your age! You need to have more of a social life!"

"I have Raider, Paris, and Gabby," Bella said. "They're who I trust. I'm happy with them. I don't need anyone else."

"Or are you making excuses because you just want to hide in your room and draw?" her mom asked, pointing to the drawing Bella was holding.

"What? No," Bella said. *Partly,* she thought.

"I think yes," her mom said. "I'll tell you this. You need to get out in the world and discover who you are. Stop hiding in your 'dragon world' and go discover yourself."

"But I already know who I am!"

"I doubt that," Bella's mom said. "I didn't fully figure out who I was until I was done with school."

That's because you're different from me, Bella thought. *You were raised as a normal child, not as a Dralerian who has to deal with battles and death.* "I'll figure it out on my own, then," Bella said. "But I want to discover it through the things I like, not with makeup and fashion and an overload of people to interact with."

"You will have to learn to accept all that," Bella's mom said. "It's the way of society."

"It's not my way!"

"It might have to become your way!"

"But it's not who I am!"

"You don't know who you are yet!"

"Maybe I know, but you don't know," Bella argued, hands folded into fists. *This is too much for me. Why tonight, of all nights, must we argue about this?!*

"Trust me, I know! I'm your mother!"

"Not my real mother!" Bella said, slapping her hand over her mouth as soon as she realized what she had said.

Her mom stared at her, eyes wide, then turned away. "I think you just need to go to bed," her mom said quietly, looking away from Bella. As she was pulling the door shut, she choked out, "Good night."

"Wait! I didn't mean to say that! Wait! I'm—" Bella said as she dashed over to the door. It shut with a SLAM. Bella stopped. "I'm . . . I'm sorry," she mumbled, walking over to her bed. She collapsed onto it, her mind whirling.

She felt like crying. *There's no point, though,* Bella thought, wiping her eyes with her hand. *She can never understand me. She adopted me after I was found at the church doorstep, where Knifeclaw dropped me off as a child after I hatched from an egg. And if she can never understand, should I even care what she thinks?*

Bella couldn't stop the tears. She let them fall onto her pillow. *Stop lying to yourself. She's still your mom, biological or not. She loves you and wants the best for you.*

I wish I could tell her about my secret, about my power, but it's too risky. I don't know if I could fully trust her to accept me. Bella sat up, blinking and wiping the tears away from her eyes. *I'll make it up to her. I'll talk to one new person at school tomorrow. That will make her at least a little happy.*

She paused and looked out the window. *What if she's right? What if the human me isn't good enough? I think I can be successful as both a dragon and a human, but what if others in the world don't accept me for who I am as a person? I know my friends appreciate me, but what about future teachers? Future bosses? Future coworkers? What if I really do need to change who I am?*

She pulled a blanket over her and lay her head on her pillow, her brown hair spreading about. She closed her eyes, trying to drift off to sleep, but thoughts and events from the day kept prodding her mind until exhaustion lulled her to sleep. However, even in her dreams, her mind echoed one thought.

Who am I supposed to be as a human?

CHAPTER 7

GEORGE

Bella burst through the doors of the school. She dashed down the hallway, past all the students, gripping the handles of the backpack on her back.

I'm running late. I'm running late, she thought, looking at a clock. *Okay, so it's 7:53. Class hasn't started yet, but I'm running later than I want to be!*

Bella continued to run. She did not see the book lying in her path. Her foot hit the book, and Bella tumbled to the ground. She pushed herself up with her hands.

"Not watching where you're going? I'm not surprised," a voice said.

Bella paused, sighing. She turned around to see a girl clad in a bright pink tank top and a black skirt. Her blue eyes pierced straight into Bella's.

Lucy, Bella thought, glaring at the girl.

"Hello, Lucy," Bella said. "It's nice to see that, even though you have some of the top grades in the school, you feel like you can leave your notebooks lying higgledy-piggledy everywhere."

"Well, it's nice to see that, even with your good grades, you will be late to class," Lucy snapped back.

"At least I wasn't wasting my time last night at the middle school dance filled to the brim with rowdy students and cliques," Bella said as she stood up, adjusting her backpack. "I got all my homework done instead."

"Good for you, doing your homework," Lucy snarked. "I got all mine done before the dance! Besides, people like seeing me at social events. Nobody wants you there, anyway, so it's a good thing you consider them a waste of time!"

"Not all social events," Bella said. "Just ones with too much chaos and too many people like you."

Lucy's blue eyes narrowed. "Makes sense that you say that," she said. "Someone with no social life, who's different from everyone else, just can't handle people like me who actually have a life! You can't handle people who have a social media feed so they actually know what's going on in the world!"

Another reason I'm glad I wasn't at the school dance, Bella thought. *Lucy and her social media are dangerous to me. If Lucy ever caught me transforming into a dragon, the whole school, the whole world, would find out my secret. She would use it all against me, just to get me in trouble.*

"I'm glad I'm not wasting all my time on some electronic device," Bella said.

"I'm glad that most of the students are already in their classrooms," a cold, deep voice sneered.

Bella looked to the side. She froze. A tall man in a suit with short black hair glared at them with cold, blue eyes.

Mr. Wellington! Bella thought. *It would have to be the strictest teacher in school who shows up right now!*

"Come on, now. It's May. You're both seventh graders, and you're both thirteen. You should have grown out of this nonsense already," Mr. Wellington said. "I'll let it go this time, but if I catch you again . . ." He looked at Bella. "After all, I'm sure you don't want to be caught in some fistfight like you were in the Bully Incident." He chuckled.

Bella grumbled to herself. *I wish people would let that event go,* she thought. *So I had to fight off some bully twice the size of me who was hurting my friends. So what? And why does everyone seem to take the bully's side, anyway?*

"What are you waiting for, an invitation? Head to class," Mr. Wellington ordered. Lucy nodded and walked away. Bella turned away.

"Wait."

Bella stopped. She looked back at Mr. Wellington. "Yes?"

"Bella, I forgot to notify you that Mr. Arden has requested to see you in his office this morning," he said. "I suggest you go there immediately."

"Yes, Mr. Wellington," Bella said, taking off at a run. She dashed down the hallway, her footsteps echoing on the smooth tile beneath her feet.

"No running in the halls, Bella!" Mr. Wellington bellowed as she ran away from him.

Thank goodness I'm far enough away from him so it looks as if I can't hear him. As she ran, she could hear locker doors shutting and the dull murmur of students talking to one another as teachers planned their day.

Oh yeah, I've got to find a student to make an acquaintance with today. I forgot how hard that's going to be. All the kids here have their own cliques. Even the kids rejected by every other clique have a clique. Plus, all the kids here think I'm too different to associate with . . .

Bella slowed down, walking up to a door with a bronze plaque that read *Principal Arden.* She took a deep breath and slowly pushed open the door. The secretary looked at her and pointed to the back office. Bella nodded and walked toward another door. She pushed it open with caution and entered the room. There at the desk sat Mr. Arden, the principal. *He's the tallest, biggest, and strongest person here in the school,* she thought, eyeing his large hands, broad shoulders, and round head. *I wouldn't be surprised if the rumors about him being a boxer are true.*

"Hello, Isabella," he said.

"Hello, Mr. Arden." *What does he want?*

"I presume Mr. Wellington sent you in here as I requested him to do?"

"Yes, sir." Bella paused, then said, "Why do you want to see me?"

"It has come to my recent attention that your grades have been better than ever, and you have been one of the best-behaved kids in school this year. Well, if you exclude the Bully Incident."

Bella rolled her eyes. *Everyone is going to know about the Bully Incident wherever I go, aren't they?*

"Never mind that. Because your grades and behavior have been top-notch, I would like to offer you an opportunity I have never offered you before."

Bella raised her eyebrows. "What is it?"

Mr. Arden stood up. "I need you to show a new student around the school today," he said. "Would you be willing to do that for me?"

Bella's eyes widened. *A new kid! Someone without a clique! Someone who doesn't know that everybody else sees me as too different! This is the perfect opportunity!* "Yes, Mr. Arden, I'd be more than willing to show a new kid around."

"Excellent!" Mr. Arden turned around and called, "George! Come in."

The door opened, and in walked the next teen model. His blond hair swished on his head, his blue eyes glinted in the light, and he was dressed in fashionable clothes. He had a strong, tough build.

Well. He's cute, Bella thought, looking him over. But her subconscious dragon-self sensed something about him. *Peculiar . . . He gives off a very warm sensation, almost like you're standing next to a scorching fire.*

This made Bella want to get away from him. Normal people did not feel like burning fires. *But I promised the principal I would do this . . . I can't quit now. Besides, it will please my mom. And it's just one day.*

"Hi! I'm Isabella Edelsten, but you can just call me Bella!" She smiled, holding out her hand.

The boy hesitated, then reached out his right hand and shook hers. "I'm . . . I'm George. George Knight."

"George, Bella will show you around the school today. Understood?" Mr. Arden said.

"Yes," George said. His voice was deep and smooth.

"You may head back to class, Bella," Mr. Arden said.

"Thank you, sir," Bella said. She beckoned George to follow her. As Bella and George walked out of the room and down the hallway, she pointed out everything to him, from lockers to signs to other classrooms. As she showed him the way, Bella thought, *You know, I wonder what would happen if George became a part of my group of friends. I wonder how that would affect the four of us.* That hot, fire-like sensation came back as she walked next to him. *Of course, I keep getting that weird feeling around him. I don't trust it. I wonder what will happen today with him around.*

She stopped in front of a classroom door. "And this is math," Bella said. "A man named Mr. Wellington teaches this class. I'll forewarn you, he's very irritable and cold." She pushed open the door.

"All right," George said.

Bella entered the classroom, George behind her. All heads in the classroom jerked up from their work to stare at this new student.

"Who is this?" Mr. Wellington demanded, pointing at George.

"I'm George Knight. I'm here to join your class," George said.

Bella heard a couple of girls laugh and swoon. Mr. Wellington glared at the class, then looked back at George. "Yes, I heard you'd start attending school today. Come here."

George walked over to Mr. Wellington's desk. "Here is your textbook," the teacher said, slapping the heavy book into George's hands. "Sit over in that empty desk."

"Thank you, sir," George said, smiling. He strode over to the desk in the corner.

Bella walked back toward her desk. Paris grinned and waved discreetly. Raider smiled at Bella. *But why isn't Gabby waving?* Bella thought, looking at her friend. *What the . . . ?* She was shocked at the sight before her. Gabby's eyes were fixed on George, her pupils were dilated, her cheeks were pinker than before, and there was a gentle, silly smile on her face.

Oh no, Bella thought, sitting down. *Just what I need. One of my friends in love.*

TAP TAP TAP. Bella looked to the right. Paris discreetly pointed at George, then Gabby, then made a gagging motion to her mouth.

Bella snickered quietly, looking back at her work. She heard a nearby cough. She looked to her left. Raider looked at her. He looked at George, then at Bella.

"What is it, Raider?" she telecommunicated to him. *Thank goodness Dralerians can still telecommunicate in human form,* she thought.

Raider winced, grabbing his head, then telecommunicated, "Who . . . is . . . he?"

"He's a new student. Mr. Arden assigned him to me today to show him around the school."

Raider looked back at George, then faced Bella. "I don't . . . trust him."

Bella looked back at George, then faced Raider. Her mind flashed back to the hot, fiery feeling she'd sensed when she'd first met him. She telecommunicated to Raider, "I don't exactly trust him either. I get this weird feeling whenever I'm around him, like I'm standing next to a bonfire. But I agreed to it, and we're stuck with him for the day. "

"All right," Raider telecommunicated back to her. "I'm just . . . worried . . . something . . . will happen."

"It's okay," Bella telecommunicated to him. "We're only with him for a day. Everything will be fine."

She glanced back at George. Something caught her eye. It was Lucy. She was eyeing George. Then she scowled at Bella, her eyes narrow.

Although, Bella thought, looking back down at her textbook, *if I just upset the school hierarchy, things might not be so fine after all.*

CHAPTER 8

THE TRIALS OF SCHOOL

CLICK!

SLAM!

The clang of lockers filled Bella's ears. She stood by her friends, placing books into her locker.

"So, George, what did you think of English?" Bella asked.

"English? It was fun, but hard," George said.

"Oh! Oh yeah, English is so hard, isn't it? I know," Gabby said, dashing over to George and nodding. George looked at Gabby with a peculiar look on his face. Bella watched as Paris facepalmed.

"I rather enjoyed phys ed," George said. "Will we do that again today?"

"No, only once a day," Bella answered, grabbing a sketchbook out of her locker.

"George, I like phys ed too! We have so much in common!" Gabby chirped.

"Yeah, you love phys ed so much you collapsed onto the ground during push-ups and told me how much you hated it afterward," Paris said.

Gabby glared at Paris, mouthing the words *shut up*. Paris only snickered.

Bella looked up. Lucy was walking by them, glaring at George and Bella. *For goodness' sake*, Bella thought, glaring back at Lucy. *What is her problem today?*

"Who is that?" George asked, watching Lucy walk away with her friends.

"Oh, that's Lucy," Bella said. "She is the most popular girl here at Red Raven Middle School. She gets good grades, and everyone loves her. She hates me, though."

"Why?"

"I honestly have no idea, but I'm not too fond of her either," Bella said, slamming her locker door shut.

George stood in silence. "I'll be right back," he said suddenly. "Wait for me, please." With a smooth stride, he took off down the hallway.

SLAM! "Bella, I don't like him," Paris said. "Get him out of here as soon as possible."

"I agree," Raider said, shutting his locker.

"I know. I don't fully trust him either," Bella said. Her mind flashed back to meeting him, when it felt like she was standing next to a bonfire.

"Yeah, I get this feeling when I'm next to him, like he's a dangerous fire or something," Raider said.

"Same!" Paris said.

"I think George is just fine," Gabby said. "More than fine. Definitely more than fine."

"That's because you fell head over heels for him!" Paris snapped.

Gabby's face turned beet-red. She immediately reached for her open locker. "I-I forgot my sketchbook," she stuttered from behind the locker door.

Well, Bella thought, *at least he'll only be sticking around us for one day. I can deal with him today to make my mom happy. After that, though, I have no idea what I'll do.* "Okay. Today will be the only day we spend time with George. Tomorrow I'll have him start hanging out with someone else. Okay?"

"Great!" Paris cheered, leaping in the air.

"Aww . . ." Gabby said. "I still want to hang out with him."

"Well, you can," Bella said, "but I think the others would prefer you to hang out with him elsewhere."

"All right," Gabby murmured, shutting her locker door.

"I'm glad he's only going to be around us one day," Raider said, facing Bella. "There's just something I sense about him," he whispered. "I just don't trust him. And if he hurt one of us . . . if he hurt you . . ." He put his hand on her shoulder. "I don't know what I would do."

Bella smiled and shrugged, feeling her face grow warm. "It will be okay."

"I'm back," a suave voice said. Bella jerked her head to the side, startled. Raider walked away from Bella and shut his locker.

"Oh, hi, George," Bella said. "Let's head to class." Bella and her friends walked down the crowded hallway, stepping between groups of kids and conversations. They pointed out more things for George, showing him their school. They came to a stop in front of a door decked out in students' artwork.

"What is this classroom? Why is the door so decorated?" George asked.

"Oh, this is Mrs. Samsworth's classroom," Bella said, pushing open the door. "She teaches art!" Bella stepped into the classroom, and bright colors met her eyes. Paintings and drawings hung on the wall, and art materials were everywhere. *This is, by far, my favorite class*, Bella thought, grinning as she sat down at her spot at a table.

"Well, Mrs. Samsworth put up more art, didn't she?" Paris said, eyeing the walls as she sat by Bella.

"So it seems," Raider said, pulling up a chair.

"Mind if I sit here?" George asked, pulling up a chair next to Bella.

"Not at all!"

"I'll sit next to you, too!" Gabby said, sitting in a chair immediately.

"Hello! Who is this?" a bright, cheerful voice asked. A teacher with multicolored hair rushed over toward them.

"Good morning, Mrs. Samsworth!" Bella said. "This is George. He's a new student here."

"Excellent!" Mrs. Samsworth said. "However, this spot is intended for another student, George. I know where an open spot is! I'll show it to you!" She beckoned him to follow her. George got up, tucking his right hand into his pant pocket. He strode away, walking close to all the tables.

"All right, class, let's begin!" Mrs. Samsworth chirped, walking to her desk. "Today, we'll be working on our portraits from yesterday. The media we'll be using is—"

The intercom crackled. "Mrs. Samsworth, please report to the principal's office. There has been an emergency with the art display case in the front hall."

Mrs. Samsworth gasped. Her face went pale. "Class, I'll be back. I trust all of you to be responsible while I'm gone. You know what you need to do." She swung the door to the classroom open.

Just as it was about to shut, she said, "Whoever sits still and behaves while I am gone gets an A." The door shut with a SLAM.

The classroom remained silent. Slowly, the scratch-scratch of pencils scraping paper filled the room. Bella looked straight at her work, a portrait of herself. *All right, time to get to work*, she thought, reaching for her drawing pencil. *I definitely want an A.*

Her hand closed on air.

She looked over at her pencil pile. *Colored pencils, erasers . . . where is my sketching pencil?* She grabbed the pencils and sorted through them. She sifted through other pencil piles on the table.

My drawing pencil isn't here. In fact, there's no other drawing pencil at this table that's not in use. She stood up.

"Where are you going?" Raider asked.

"To find my pencil. It's missing." She walked away, toward Mrs. Samsworth's desk. *Thank goodness there's a spare pencil pile*—her thought stopped when she glanced to the side. She was looking at Lucy's desk.

Lucy had her pencil.

Oh, that no-good little . . . Bella stormed over to Lucy's desk. *She's been a brat to me all day. Now she takes my pencil! What is wrong with her?* She stood right in front of Lucy, looking down at her. "AHEM," Bella coughed.

Lucy looked up, then grimaced. "What do you want?"

"What do I want? Well, you should know."

"Why should I know? I've been sitting here the whole time."

"Ugh." Bella sighed. "Just give up already. You took my pencil to aggravate me." Bella reached her hand toward her pencil.

SLAP! Lucy whacked Bella's reaching hand with her own hand. "What is the meaning of this? I didn't take your stupid pencil! Go grab another pencil, or ask your hot boyfriend to give you one of his!"

"Hot boyfriend? I have no hot boyfriend! Give me my pencil! That's all I want!" Bella demanded, pointing at her pencil and sticking out her right hand.

Lucy looked at Bella's pencil and grimaced. "Fine. Fine! You know what? Take your dumb pencil," Lucy snapped, throwing Bella's pencil at her face. Bella's hands shot up and blocked the pencil. It bounced down to the floor.

"Couldn't you have just handed the pencil to me?" Bella grumbled. She looked from Lucy to the class around her. *Great, now everyone's watching us!* Bella thought as she scowled.

"Oh, I could have. I could have also called your hot boyfriend over here to give it to you," Lucy snapped, standing up. "Would you have preferred that instead?"

"What hot boyfriend?!"

"Oh, I don't know, the dreamboat over in the corner?" Lucy pointed to George. "You're one of the biggest outsiders in this whole school. The only things you care about are your weird friends and dragons. Yet you still get good grades, the teachers still like you, and now you have a hot man wrapped around your finger! Do you have any idea how hard I work for an opportunity like that? And Mr. Arden chose YOU for it instead, of all people," she spat.

"Wait . . . you're jealous of me?!" Bella exclaimed. Images of hiding secrets, transforming into Emer, and all the bloodshed she had seen flashed into her mind. *How could Lucy, queen of the Red Raven Middle School, be jealous of me?*

"Jealous?" Lucy spat, the slightest hint of worry on her face. "I'm not jealous!"

"All I'm trying to do is fit in," Bella said. "Trying to make new friends. All that kind of stuff, you know."

Lucy laughed a shrill, high laugh, brushing the blonde hair out of her face. "You? Fit in? Ha!"

Bella's heart sank in her chest. "Why? Why couldn't I fit in?" she demanded.

"You're asking ME why you'll never fit in?" Lucy hissed, approaching Bella. Bella backed away, but Lucy continued to corner her. "You're weird. You're different. You still believe in imaginary childhood creatures. You use no social media at all. You're not trendy. You don't talk with anyone. You draw WAY too much, and to top it all off, you give me a bad vibe!"

"But if I changed all that, would I fit in?" Bella asked.

"You will NEVER FIT IN WITH US! The whole WORLD!" Lucy yelled. "No one besides your dopey friends will accept you!"

Bella felt as if a knife stabbed her in the heart. *Why? I just wanted to make my mom happy. But . . .* Her thoughts swirled, and she couldn't sort anything out. She backed away from Lucy again. Her foot caught on the back of a chair. Bella lost her balance and tumbled backward onto the desk. The sound of clattering plastic and metal filled the classroom as the desk fell sideways, hitting the ground. Bella looked up. The whole classroom was staring at her and Lucy.

The door opened. "What is going on in here?" a voice demanded. Bella looked at the door. *Mrs. Samsworth,* Bella thought. *This is not good.*

"Bella! And Lucy! Misbehaving while I was gone!" Mrs. Samsworth said, walking into the classroom. "Shame on the two of you!" She yanked up Bella by the arm. "Bella, wait out there." She pointed outside of the classroom.

"Yes," Bella muttered, walking out of the classroom. *Why does this have to happen to me? I know I'm partly at fault, but couldn't Lucy have just handed over the pencil? Why was it so hard for her to do that?*

Something caught Bella's eye. *What's that?* She walked over toward the object. It was a notebook. However, it was not an ordinary notebook. *It's got a leather cover and a thin leather-string binding,* Bella thought, picking up the notebook. *It looks like the one I've got back in the Bluescale cave. I wonder whose it is?* She flipped through the pages. *Surely someone's written a name—*

She froze. Her heart stopped in her chest. Her hands froze on a page in the notebook.

But . . . this can't be. How can this—

"All right, Lucy! Let's get going!" Mrs. Samsworth snapped, dragging Lucy out of the classroom. Bella tucked the small notebook into a pocket inside her jacket.

"Come on, Bella, what are you waiting for?" Mrs. Samsworth grabbed Bella's wrist and steered her down the hallway as well. "Let's see what the principal will say about this."

But at that moment, Bella didn't care. Her mind was focused on the object drawn in the notebook.

The Dark Energy Crystal.

That drawing can't just be a coincidence. I've seen the Crystal with my own eyes, and it looks exactly like that. That can only mean one thing.

Someone in this school knows about the Dark Energy Crystal.

This is terrible.

CHAPTER 9

STONEHORN'S SORROW

Well, today was just dandy, wasn't it?

Bella was lying on her bed at home, her arms and legs sprawled out on the blankets.

I got suspended over a pencil.

A PENCIL.

She thought back to her meeting in the principal's office.

"What do you mean, you got in a fight?" Mr. Arden's voice had boomed in her ears.

"Lucy took my pencil, and I asked for her to give it back," Bella had said. "She didn't, and then things took a turn for the worse."

"So you started the fight?"

"Well, perhaps. I asked her for the pencil."

"You started the fight."

"We never got physical. It was only verbal."

"A fight is a fight!"

So he was mad because Lucy and I were mean to each other, and he suspended Lucy for two days and me for a week because our arguing 'endangered' the students. Bella sulked. *Verbal arguing between students does not, for the most part, endanger other students!*

Bella sat up, throwing her pillow to the side. *Mom wasn't happy she had to come pick me up. I got to hear all about fitting in again, too,* Bella thought, sighing. *I know I got in trouble. I know I'm different. But I'm trying my best.*

Of course, the biggest thing to worry about is the fact that someone in the school knows about the Dark Energy Crystal. But who? I texted my friends about it. None of them have a notebook like that, nor do they draw things like that. Could it be George? That'd be too much of a coincidence, though.

Bella looked out the window. The warm sunlight gleamed, and cirrus clouds seemed to glide across the bright blue sky. The faint spring breeze tickled the trees, rustling their newly budded leaves.

It's such a pretty day. She was tempted. She was more than tempted. *Well, I could use something to clear my head,* she thought, leaping out of bed and walking to her window. She unclicked the locks and slid the window open. Bella gripped the windowsill and pushed herself up, and then her feet landed on the wooden frame beneath her. She glanced to the side. The silver rain gutter gleamed from the sunbeams reflecting from it. *Okay, you can do this,* Bella thought, crouching lower. *You've done this countless times before. One . . . two . . .*

Three! Bella leaped off the windowsill. She flew through the air, straight toward the long, silver pipe. CLANG! Bella grabbed on to the slick metal pipe, arms gripping and wrapping around the rain gutter. She slid to the ground, her hair flying up in the air. Finally, her feet landed on soft grass. Bella let go of the pipe, looking at the ground, then walked farther out in the yard to look at her room. *I know I can fly as a dragon, but I do worry about hurting myself when pulling stunts like that in human form.*

Bella walked to the center of her yard; the cool grass tickled her bare feet. *No one is in the neighborhood. They're all at work or school. I'm safe.*

She placed her right hand to her heart. Bright light flashed around her. She grew shiny blue scales on her arms, and yellow-gold talons sprouted on her fingers. Small yellow spikes sprouted down her back. Her hair turned into yellow-gold curved horns. Two wings sprouted out of her back, her tail lashed behind her, and chest plates appeared on her chest. A bright green emerald flashed onto the center of her chest.

She was now Emer, the Bluescale warrior.

Emer leaped into the sky, wings beating the air around her. The sun gleamed on her scales, warming her. She twirled in the air, flying up by the clouds. She looked at the ground. *Everything looks so small. It's nice to fly. It allows me to see how small the world really is, how small my worries are.*

Her eyes caught on something. It was blood-red, with black wings and silver spines. It held something blue in its talons.

A Bloodclaw.

Emer folded in her wings, diving toward the red drag-on. The air whistled in her ears. She swooped by the Blood-claw. It screeched at her, breathing a torrent of flames.

It's a crabby Bloodclaw, Emer thought. *Looks like it wants to eat something, too.* She eyed the pale-blue drag-on in its back talons.

The Bloodclaw lunged at her, swiping its shiny black talons at her. She dodged the attack, swooping around the Bloodclaw. Emer breathed a plume of green flames at the Bloodclaw's head. It eyed the flames, whipping its head away from them.

Emer dived in, ramming the Bloodclaw in the stomach. "SCREEEEEECH!" It flew backward through the air. It lost its grip on its meal, which tumbled away. Emer flapped her wings, chasing the falling dragon. She caught it in her talons.

"HISSSSS!" The Bloodclaw charged at her. Emer growled, waiting for it to fly closer. The Bloodclaw was feet away from her. She blasted a stream of green fire at the Bloodclaw. The flames caught on the Bloodclaw's scales, burning it. Its wingbeats slowed, and it collapsed, falling through the air to the ground below.

Emer let out a breath of air. She looked at the dragon she had caught in her talons. *It's a Pinescale,* Emer thought, eyeing the large, triangular scales of the small dragon. *Though I've never seen one in this color. I've read they're all green and brown, not blue and yellow.* She gently touched the dragon's pale-blue scales, which were covered in cuts and blood.

"Stonehorn!" Emer telecommunicated.

"Yes?" Stonehorn's voice rang in her head.

"I need help! I just saved an injured Pinescale from a Blood-claw, and it needs someone to tend to its injuries right away!"

"No problem," Stonehorn said. Emer looked up and around. Stonehorn was diving toward her, and then he spread his light-yellow wings out and hovered in place. Another Bluescale was flying with him. Her dark-blue scales glinted in the sunlight as she hovered next to Stonehorn.

"Stonehorn! How did you get here so fast?" Emer asked.

"I've been training a fellow Cavedweller how to scout outside the cave in desperate times," Stonehorn said. "Indigo! We must bring back this hurt dragon!"

"Yes, Stonehorn!" the female Bluescale responded. She held out her foretalons. Emer placed the small, wounded Pinescale in Indigo's claws.

"Perfect! Expert patient handling, Indigo!" Stonehorn said.

"Thanks." Indigo grinned.

"Let's head back. That little dragon is in dire need of care," he said.

"Actually," Emer said, "Stonehorn, could you stay here for a minute? I'd like to talk with you about something."

His eyes widened. He looked from Emer to his student. "Indigo, can you find your way back to the cave with the injured Pinescale?"

"Yes," Indigo said, looking from Emer to Stonehorn. "I'll telecommunicate with you when I drop off the patient in Vladmir's cave." She flicked her tail and flew away, wings beating rapidly.

"Let's go down there," Emer said. She dived down toward the ground and landed in a field of prairie grass. She scanned her surroundings. *No humans in sight. Good.*

"Oof!" Stonehorn said, stumbling as he landed. He shook his head. "So . . . uh . . . what would you like to discuss?"

"How is Skye doing? Have you checked up on him?" Emer asked.

The bright gleam in Stonehorn's eyes disappeared. "Skye . . . lost part of his left forearm. Physically, he's doing better, but emotionally . . . he's devastated. He's disappointed beyond words. He refuses to talk with anyone, including me. He's blocking out the world." He sighed. "I wish I could help him."

Emer winced, then said, "At least he survived."

"Unlike my father," Stonehorn said, eyes narrowing. "Why didn't you tell me he died?"

Emer hesitated. "You were really upset. I didn't want to upset you more."

"Of course," he said, staring at the ground. "As if it weren't bad enough that Father and I argued that morning, he died later that day!" Tears dripped out of his eyes. "I feel like scum. Pond scum."

"You're not scum," Emer said, brushing her wing against his. "Sometimes, things in life happen. If you need to, you could take a break from your duties for a few days. It would help you recover from this ordeal."

"I'm not taking a break," Stonehorn said. "I'm a Cavedweller; my duty is to help others. There are many Bluescales that need help in the cave, and I must help them, whether

I'm struggling or not. I must be strong."

"Are you sure?"

"Positive."

"All right," Emer said, gazing up at the sky. After a pause, she said, "If you don't mind me asking, what were you and Battlescar arguing about, anyway? You don't have to answer if you don't want to."

Stonehorn looked at the ground. "My father was mad because I'm a Cavedweller," he said. "He always hated the fact I chose to be a Cavedweller instead of a guard or a warrior. Yesterday morning, he was going to show Skye to his new rank in the cave, as his apprentice. Father told me that I should be more like that and not just hide in the Bluescale cave and do chores. I argued with him, saying that it was important and that I preferred to help others instead of fight. He didn't listen, and kept insulting me. I . . . I . . ."

Emer looked at Stonehorn. His pale-blue eyes focused on hers.

"I told him that I wished he wasn't my father," Skye growled, looking back at the ground.

Emer's eyes widened. Her wings drooped.

"I feel more than terrible now," Stonehorn said. "If I had known what was to happen later on that day, how he would die . . ." Stonehorn breathed out a bit of smoke. "But no one will understand. No one seems to understand how hard it is to argue with your parent."

"I do," Emer said.

"You do? But how?" Stonehorn asked. "All the elders here at the Bluescale cave love you and respect you. No one would dare to disagree with you!"

"My mother believes I should change myself so I can fit in more with human society," Emer said. "Start following more human fashion, become more social with strangers, all that kind of stuff."

"Why, I hope you'd never change yourself!" Stonehorn sputtered. "You're delightful just the way you are!"

"Yeah," Emer said. "But there are others who want me to change, too. It might be inevitable."

"Nothing is inevitable; not with you, at least." Stonehorn smiled. "You will find some way to fix it. You are Emer the Dralerian warrior, slayer of Bloodclaws, bringer of justice, leader of the Chosen Ones!"

Emer laughed. "Thanks. You're right. I'll find a solution to my dilemma. I know you will find one, too."

He looked at her, smile fading away. "But how?"

"Well, I'd try to reach out more to your brother," Emer said.

"But what about the past? What about my issue with my father?"

"I think . . . I think your father forgives you," Emer said. "I think that now, up in the Great Sky Above with the Greatwing, he knows how you feel. He's probably been watching you. I think he understands. I think that now what he would want you to do is watch after your brother and care for him. He's the only living member of your family left, and your father knows you will protect him."

Stonehorn stared at Emer. His face slowly turned to a smile. "Thanks, Emer," he said, brushing his wing against hers. "You truly are a hero to all."

"You're welcome." Emer smiled.

Stonehorn looked up at the sky. "Goodness! So much time has passed! I'd better be on my way." He unfurled his large wings. "See you soon," he said, launching off the ground, flapping his wings, and taking off into the sky.

"Bye," Emer called out. She launched off the ground, catching the wind in her wings and gliding back toward her house.

It's a pity I can't go to the Bluescale cave tonight. I wish I could see that little dragon recover. But my mother will be home tonight, and she'll want to spend time with me, probably giving me ways to change myself 'for the better.' She sighed, letting the wind push her forward. *Well, I got to talk with Stonehorn some. I hope I made him feel a little better. At least I resolved one issue at hand.*

But there are many more, Emer thought, her mind nagging her. *The Bloodclaws are suddenly attacking again. I got suspended from school. Someone in school knows about the Dark Energy Crystal, and there are people that keep telling me that I'll never fit in. I want to be myself, but people keep telling me that who I am isn't good enough.*

I know I can attack those Bloodclaws, but where will they strike next? Who does that notebook belong to? Should I really try to change my human side?

Emer shut her eyes, exhaling, letting the sun shine on her scales. *I told Stonehorn what to do. I gave him the answers he needed. I just wish I knew what to do about my own problems.*

CHAPTER 10

THAT NAGGING FEELING

BRRRRRRINNNNNG!

The sounds of stampeding feet, yelling kids, and locker doors slamming filled Raider's ears. He winced.

"Ah, thank goodness class is done!" Paris said, exhaling dramatically. "Finally, I can have some fun!"

"Oh, that's tonight, isn't it?" Raider said, looking at Paris. She nodded. *Bella texted me and said that tonight was the night we could go to the Bluescale cave, because her mom will be working at the hospital the whole night,* Raider thought. *It works for Paris and me, too. My mom's out of town, and Paris's mom is always busy.*

"You know, it sure is weird without Bella here in school," Paris said, her locker door opening with a CLICK.

"Yeah," Raider said. "She was suspended yesterday, right?"

"Yes. Yesterday was Wednesday, and today's Thursday. Shouldn't you know that, Raider? Aren't you a little crazy when it comes to scheduling stuff?"

"Well, I haven't been keeping track much lately," Raider admitted, scratching his head.

Paris looked at Raider as she slammed her locker door shut. "Oh my gosh," she said. "You only do and say all your obnoxious scheduling stuff because it gets Bella's attention, don't you?"

"What! No," Raider said, looking away from Paris. "Why would I do that?"

"Hello, everyone," a suave voice interrupted. Raider looked over his shoulder. *Well, for once George came at a good time.* George's left arm was slung around Gabby's shoulders, and she was grinning from ear to ear.

"What's going on?" Paris asked, raising an eyebrow.

"George is taking me to the local fro-yo shop." Gabby giggled.

"Yes, so we can eat fro-yo together," George said, glancing around.

"Ugh," Raider muttered, opening his locker. *So much for getting rid of George after his first day here. Ever since George asked if Gabby could show him around the school again, she's been keeping him close by her side. It's also been kind of uncomfortable to watch them,* he thought, shoving some books into his locker. *I think there's something not right about that kid, and to watch him butter up one of my friends . . .*

"George, what are you doing?" Gabby asked.

Raider peeked around his locker door to see George walking around, eyeing the ground.

"I'm just missing something," he said, grinning at Gabby.

"The same object as you were yesterday?"

"Yes. I'll be back." He walked down the hallway through the crowds of kids scattered about.

"Mmm, he's so hot," Gabby murmured.

"Is that all that matters? What about nice? And smart? And funny?" Paris asked.

"Those, too."

"Gabby," Raider said, walking out from behind his locker door, "I don't think you should go out with him tonight."

"What! Why?"

"Because he's not to be trusted," Paris snapped, walking over by them. "Besides, we're all going together with Bella tonight, remember?"

"He can be trusted! I trust him!"

"How well do you know him?" Raider demanded. "It's been one day, Gabby. You've known him one day. What if he's not who you think he is?"

"He is who I think he is!" Gabby said.

"You never know," Paris muttered.

"Listen to me!" Gabby exclaimed. "I know George. I know him with my whole heart. We are soul mates! We're meant to be together!" She crossed her arms. "Tell Bella I say hi, but I'll be with George tonight, because I love him."

"Gabby, I'm back," George said, walking up beside her. She grinned, blushing. "Let's head to that fro-yo place, shall we?"

"Yes!" she said. The two walked toward the school doors, holding hands as if they didn't have a care in the world.

Raider clenched his teeth. *If only Bella were here. She could stop this. She could convince Gabby that George isn't the best for her. If only I had some power . . .*

"What's up? You're deep in thought, I can tell," Paris said, hoisting her backpack on her shoulders.

"I just wish Bella were here."

"So you could annoy her with more scheduling stuff?"

"No!" Raider said, face growing hot. "No. Because she's like the leader of our group, in a way. She could convince Gabby to avoid George, whereas I have almost no power in that matter."

"You seem to have no power here or there," she said.

"Hey! I'll get my element soon!" he whispered.

"I can't wait until I'm powerful," Paris said quietly, a smile on her face. "Then maybe I could stand in the way of George."

"Yes," Raider said, "but we must be quiet about this, okay? Let's not talk about powers anymore."

"Fine," Paris said.

Raider pushed open the door to the school, holding it open. *There's been a lot going on this week*, he thought. *First, a Bloodclaw attack, then George came to our school, then Bella was suspended, and now George and Gabby are . . . dating? I don't know.*

He let go of the door, walking next to Paris on the sun-warmed concrete. *I know I shouldn't be worried. It's ridiculous to be worried. George is just some normal kid, at a normal school. I shouldn't be worried, right?*

But then, why didn't Bella and Paris like him either?

Why do I not trust him?

Why does this not feel right?

CHAPTER 11

LESSONS LEARNED

Bella sat, waiting.

Where are they? she thought, looking at her phone. *It's almost five o'clock. Raider, Paris, and Gabby should be here now. Did they forget?*

She smiled. *No, my friends wouldn't forget. Raider schedules everything, and Paris loves the Bluescale cave, and Gabby always wants to hang out with me.*

The wind blew in her face. The fields of long prairie grass rustled in the gusts of wind. Pebbles on the barren road tumbled about, and the old wooden bench she sat on squeaked.

The pitter-patter of feet caught her attention. She looked up and smiled.

"Raider! Paris!" she called out, bolting off the bench.

"Bella!" they answered, dashing toward her. She ran

toward them. She slowed as they all approached one another, grinning and gasping for breath.

"Hey! How have you been, you lucky duck, getting all those days off from school?" Paris asked, chuckling.

"I wouldn't call myself lucky," Bella said, glancing around. "Where's Gabby?"

Raider grimaced. Paris barked a sharp laugh. "Wouldn't you like to know," Paris said, walking forward.

"What? What's going on?" Bella asked, walking with her friends toward the worn-down bench.

"Gabby didn't want to come with us tonight," Raider said.

"Because she's going on a date with Mr. Perfect!" Paris said.

"Gabby is going on a date with George?" Bella asked, brushing aside stalks of long grass.

"Yeah. It's ridiculous, isn't it?" Paris said, crossing her arms.

"We've tried to tell her not to, but she won't listen," Raider said.

"This is peculiar," Bella said. "I mean, I guess I don't completely mind her dating George, but I'd wait to know him better. She should wait."

"Yes! I know!" Paris agreed, kicking the long grass.

"School has been interesting lately," Raider said. "I wish you were there, though."

"Thanks." Bella smiled. She glanced around. "Okay, I think we're out far enough. Raider, we can transform now."

"Got it."

Bella and Raider placed their hands to their hearts. Bright light flashed around them. Within a minute, their human selves had been replaced by shining scales, gleaming chest plates, large wings, curling horns, and sleek yellow-gold talons.

Bella was now Emer; Raider was now Saphir.

"You guys are so lucky to be able to do that." Paris sighed, looking at Emer's emerald and Saphir's sapphire.

"You will get the ability to do it someday," Emer said, crouching. "Hop on. We've got a lot of work to do in the Bluescale cave today. I'll work with Saphir on his training. Paris, would you be willing to check on Skye and another dragon I rescued today?"

Paris crawled onto Emer's back. "Sure," Paris said. "Wait, when did you rescue another dragon?"

"Long story," Emer said, leaping off the ground and spreading her wings. She and Saphir lifted into the air, soaring off into the bright-blue sky.

* * * * *

Paris walked down the cool gray hallways of the Bluescale cave.

It's really quiet in here, Paris thought, glancing around. *All the Bluescales must be eating now. At least that made it easier for Emer to fly up the Flight Tunnels.*

She spotted the door to Vladmir's cave and walked toward it. *Emer and Saphir are so lucky they get to train for battle right now. I wish I had my dragon form so I could do that. I don't even need my dragon form. If I could go practice battling, I'd be happy.*

She knocked on the large stone door in front of her. It creaked open. Vladmir peeked outside, looking down at her.

"Ah, Paris! Welcome!" he said, smiling. "Come in!"

Paris walked into the room. *There are certainly a lot of things in here that catch your eye,* Paris thought, eyeing the many colored GlowCrystals, the copper pot in the corner, the shelves of books, and the herbs hanging from the ceiling. "Vladmir, I am here on Gemstone Warrior business."

"Your little club!" He grinned. "Yes, it does seem to be helping you four, the Chosen Ones! The Foretelling will come true with the four of you!"

"Actually, there are only three of us here today," Paris said. "I'm here to check on two injured dragons. Skye and . . . some very scaly light-blue dragon Emer rescued? Emer said it was called a Pinescale?"

"Oh, you mean Scalene!" Vladmir said. "She's doing well. Follow me. You can't go in and see her, but I'll show you how she looks." He walked forward, pushing open another door. Paris followed him down a long hallway filled with purple GlowCrystals and small caves.

"Scalene? That's her name?" Paris asked. The image of a triangle appeared in her mind.

"She is named that due to her scales," Vladmir said, coming to a stop. "She is a Pinescale, and they often have names that associate with scales." He held out his left foretalon. "Hop on. I will show her to you."

Paris climbed up on his claw, and he lifted her into the air. She soon found herself staring through a bumpy glass window into a small cave. Inside, a dragon a little bigger than herself lay on a small blanket. Her scales were covered in bandages.

"She was caught by a Bloodclaw, poor little creature," Vladmir said, lowering his claw. "She told me she was mighty and strong, but the Bloodclaw still got her. It's lucky that Emer rescued her, or else she would have become dinner."

"I wish I could have helped," Paris said.

"How could you have helped?" Vladmir asked, tilting his head.

Paris gritted her teeth and said, "I could have distracted the Bloodclaw. I could have injured it with a rock or sharp stick. Or, if I had my dragon form, I could have helped fight off the Bloodclaw."

"You will have your dragon form when you are ready," Vladmir said patiently. "You are almost ready, but not quite. Wait a little longer."

Hmm, Scalene and I might have something in common: being underestimated, Paris thought, sighing at his answer. She hopped off his claw.

"Right over here is Skye's room," Vladmir said, walking to another stone door and opening it with care. "He is doing much better than a few days ago. Go talk with him!"

Paris eyed Vladmir, whose purple eyes glistened with kindness and eagerness. "All right," she said. "For the Gemstone Warriors."

"For the Gemstone Warriors!" Vladmir cheered.

Paris sighed, entering the room. Her eyes immediately focused on Skye. His pale-blue scales had patches of bruises and also white fabric bandages plastered on his wounds. Paris's eyes widened at his bandaged stump, which used to be his left forearm.

It's no longer there. He lost it, she thought, feeling sympathy for the young dragon. "Hello! I am Paris of the Gemstone Warriors. I wanted to check on you, see how you're doing and if you're feeling better."

"How do you think I'm feeling?" he growled, cold sky-blue eyes narrowing.

"That's what I'm waiting for you to tell me."

Skye snorted, lying down on his blanket. "Father was right," he muttered, "these human-form Chosen Ones have the brains of a rock."

"Hey, hey, hey," Paris said, "I came to check on you, not to listen to insults get thrown at me or my friend Gabby."

"Well, have you ever fought before in battle, O wise human?" Skye asked, scorn in his voice. "Have you ever trained?"

"As a matter of fact, yes. I've fought off three Bloodclaws with rocks, breaking two Bloodclaws' horns and hitting one's snout. I've been training lots, too, so I'll be ready for my dragon form."

Skye chuckled. "Look at that, a high-ranker in our society, and you're not even a dragon yet," he said. "Still a human."

Paris clenched her hands into fists. "Listen, Skye, I don't know half of what you're blabbing about, but I'm working hard, all right? Do you have a problem with me or something?"

Skye's wings flared out, and he struggled up on his haunches, glaring at her. "Do I have a problem? Of course

I have a problem! You're nothing but a pathetic human who sauntered into the cave on the back of Emer, then suddenly we find out you're a Chosen One from the Foretelling? You immediately became a High Rank! Now, most dragons admire you and look up to you, and you did nothing to earn that position! Whereas I have trained since I could stand to protect, to fight. I finally earned my role as a High Rank, and on my first day of assisting, Bloodclaws attacked! I lost everything! My new guard friends, the Dark Energy Crystal, my father, my ranking, my role in the cave . . . I can no longer fight or participate in battle activities due to my forearm."

Paris stared at the crippled dragon. Her heart suddenly ached for the poor Bluescale.

"But what do you care?" he snorted, a puff of smoke drifting out of his nose. "You've had everything handed to you on a silver platter. You'll never know the pain, the agony, the sadness. You'll never know what it's like."

Paris shuffled her feet and glanced at the ground. Past memories flashed into her mind. *Should I tell him or not?* She looked into his eyes. There were drops of tears glistening there as his eyes filled with sadness, pain, and fear.

I will tell him.

"Skye," Paris said, speaking more quietly than before, "I do know what it's like."

Skye snorted.

"My father was in the military, which is like being a guard," Paris explained. "He was a brave, strong man. He started off low-ranked, and he had to work his way up. Finally, he was a high-ranked soldier. He'd show me all his

medals, and tell me the stories of how he earned them."
She laughed, grinning.

"So your human father protected humans. How is this
supposed to help me feel—"

"He died."

The small cave suddenly became quiet. Skye paused,
mouth open. He shut it slowly, staring at Paris.

"My father died in battle," Paris said, rubbing her arm.
"He left my whole family alone."

Skye shuffled his wings.

"That is why I understand what you're going through.
I've lived with someone who's had high ranking; I've dealt
with the death of a loved one. My father dying is one reason I want to get my dragon form, so I can learn why he
wanted to protect everyone so badly."

"But if you don't know why you protect, why do you
think you'll be given a dragon form easily?" Skye asked. "I
don't know if Vladmir will let you do that."

Paris looked Skye straight in the eye. "That is what I will
find out."

Skye flicked his tail and shuffled his wings, glancing
around.

"All right, fine, you're going to be quiet," Paris said,
turning around toward the door. "You seem to be doing
much better, so—"

"Thanks."

Paris paused. She turned around to face Skye. He
looked at her, then the ground.

"I just wanted to thank you for . . . um . . . helping me out and telling me all that stuff," Skye said.

Paris looked at him, then smiled. "You're welcome." She walked toward the door, reaching for it, then stopped and looked over her shoulder. "Skye."

"What?"

"I think you'll be able to fight again."

Skye looked at her, wide-eyed. Then he smiled. It was the toothiest, happiest smile Paris had seen a dragon give.

"Thanks for having faith in me," he said.

"You're welcome," she answered. Paris pushed on the stone door with all her might. It creaked open a crack. She stepped out into the hallway, her mind feeling foggier than usual.

"Well, how did it go?" a voice asked.

"AAAARGH!" Paris jumped. "Vladmir, don't scare me like that!"

"Ah, I didn't mean to," he said, swishing his tail.

Paris eyed him closely. *His grin is bigger than usual. He knows something. He may be old and wise, but he eavesdrops.*

"Let us head out, shall we?" he said, walking forward. "Now, what would you do if you were made a Dralerian? Who and what would you protect, and why?"

Paris paused, thinking. *It's a trick question.* "Well, I'd protect my friends. I'd protect the Dark Energy Crystal, you know, when we get it back. I'd protect everyone in this cave . . . I think that's it."

"How come?"

Paris searched her mind for an answer. Her mind was blank. "Duty? I don't know," she admitted.

The two of them walked through Vladmir's cave, where the copper pot was bubbling. "Well," Vladmir said, "I think you'll figure it out soon." He patted her on the back with one of his talons.

Paris stood alert; it felt as if sparks of electricity shot through her with his touch. She quickly shook off the feeling and looked up at Vladmir. "I have to head back to the Gemstone Warriors' cave. I have to practice battling!"

Vladmir chuckled. "You do that, young one," he said, opening the door. "For with your battle practice and your confidence, you will change the world!"

"Thanks!" Paris said, walking out of the cave and waving to him. "Bye!"

"Good-bye!" Vladmir called out, smiling. The door to his cave shut with a THUD.

Paris skipped down the hallway, feeling lighthearted and happy, knowing that she had already made someone's world a better place.

CHAPTER 12

THE BATTLE OF FRIENDS

Saphir walked down the wide, tall, stone hallway. Blues-cales walked beside him, talking about food and hunting and humans, all a monotonous blur to him. All Saphir cared about was following Emer to the Gemstone Warriors' meeting cave.

"We are getting close to where it's located, right?" Saphir asked, ducking out of the way of a wing.

"It's right over here!" Emer said, pushing on a stone door and disappearing into the room. Saphir dashed over and charged into the room.

"Geez," he said, shaking his claws. "Too bad there are no Flight Tunnels in this location. My talons are sore."

"Mine are as well," Emer said.

"You know, have you ever come to think about how we dragons have big wings to fly everywhere, and we just walk underground? Doesn't that seem odd? Don't any other Bluescales' claws get sore?" Saphir pondered.

"Yeah," Emer said, "but we're used to sore talons. Living underground is what we have to do to survive. Otherwise, the Bloodclaws or humans will kill us."

"True," Saphir agreed, scanning the cave. "Hey, the large rocks are gone. And we've got GlowCrystals on the walls."

"Oh, good," Emer said. "The Cavedwellers got in here and fixed up the room yesterday. I'll have to find something to give them to thank them."

Saphir lifted one of his talons. Tiny pebbles were imbedded in his sapphire-blue scales. "It's true they worked a lot," Saphir said, "but there are certainly a lot of pebbles everywhere."

"Let's tidy up a little, then," Emer said, shrugging. She swept her tail against the ground, sweeping the surrounding pebbles into a small cluster.

Saphir eyed her, doing his best to copy her movements. He swished his tail against the ground. Again. And again. *Turns out, sweeping a floor with your tail is harder than you'd think*, he thought, flicking it in the air, shaking away the small pebbles stuck in his scales.

But he continued to watch Emer and copy her to the best of his ability, finally managing to sweep some pebbles into the pile. By then, however, most of the work had been done, and the cave was clean.

"That's done. Good!" Emer said.

"Now we'll train?"

"Now we'll train. How about we work on some physical battling skills?" Emer said, holding up her foreclaws.

"As long as you don't hurt me," Saphir said, a small grin on his face.

"I promise you that I won't," she said. "How about you make the first move?"

"All right." He paused, thinking. He swept his right talon forward, pretending to hit Emer.

"Good!" she swept her right talon as well, and swished her tail. He blocked both attacks and swiped his left talon at her. She blocked and flared her wings, leaping forward at him. He dashed out of the way, poking his talons at her side.

"You know," he said, spreading his wings and leaping above Emer, "it's very interesting."

"Why is it interesting?" Emer said, swiping a claw at him.

"Well, you chose to do physical training over elemental training. Why is that?" He swept his tail at her, and she grabbed it in her talons.

"Because I think you've had enough elemental training with Knifeclaw lately," Emer said, swiping at his face.

"All right," he said, flapping his wings and twisting away from her. He grappled the ground beneath him, thinking. "But I can't just do and know physical moves in a battle. I am going to have to find my element."

Emer sighed, flexing her claws. "You will find your element. Trust me. I know it will show up."

"But what if it doesn't?" Saphir said. "It hasn't come for four weeks. What if it never does?"

"Saphir, it will come," Emer said, charging at him.

"So far, it hasn't," Saphir said, lunging at her and grabbing her claws. "Every dragon looks down on me in this colony because I don't have an element. You don't know how that feels!"

"Really? I don't know what it feels like to be ridiculed because I don't have something everyone expects me to have?" Emer growled, shoving him to the ground. Saphir caught himself and spread his wings. "Be grateful that people appreciate you in your human form, where you don't need to worry about an element!" she said.

"I told you that you can be both dragon and human!" Saphir snarled, ramming his horns toward her.

"I am! I know!" Emer roared, leaping above him. "But it seems as if every human I know wants me to change my interests! Be someone else!" She bounded to the ground with a gentle THUD, facing Saphir.

"Well, you should be grateful the dragons admire you!" Saphir yelled, circling Emer. "Everyone keeps pressuring me to be as good as you! As strong as you!"

Saphir lunged at Emer. Emer lunged at Saphir. Their claws met with violent force. Saphir felt himself fly backward and tumble to the ground, rolling across the smooth, cool floor. He shook his head and wobbled up on his claws, sitting on his haunches. He looked over at Emer; she was sitting up as well.

She shook her head and looked at him. "I guess we're both having issues with our less-used forms, aren't we?" Her voice was quiet.

"Yeah." Saphir stood up, flicked his tail, and walked toward the door.

"Where are you going?" Emer asked.

"I just need to clear my head," he said, pulling open the stone door.

"I'm sorry if I upset you," she said, standing up immediately. "I'll come with you! I—"

"No," Saphir said. Emer looked at him, her glimmering brown eyes filled with worry.

"What? Why are you—"

"I just need some time alone," he said, walking out of the room. He could hear Emer say something, but the door shut, blocking out all verbal communication.

I hate to do that to her, Saphir thought, *but I need a break. Everyone keeps telling me my element will come, but it hasn't. They put pressure on me to find my element, but I can't find it.* He grabbed a crumpled piece of paper as he approached a small door. He pushed the door open, walking up the staircase within.

It's just hard to be a complete beginner at something and to have no idea what you're doing when everyone expects perfection. I feel as if I have no value unless I have an element.

Saphir looked up. There was a hole in the rocky ceiling above him covered by a stone on the ground above it. He reached up and pushed it away. Saphir climbed up through the hole, walking around outside on the top of the Bluescale cave. He sat down, watching the sky. Splashes of color still lit the sky's edges, but night was descending. Bright, twinkling, silver stars glimmered against their dark background.

I'm glad I found this secret exit, Saphir thought, a small smile on his face. *The Badlands and Black Hills of South*

Dakota are beautiful when viewed from here, especially during the night.

He looked down and frowned, grabbing a nearby pebble and scratching it on the paper. *Although, what value will this view have if I keep running here just for an escape? What if this place just becomes the last spot of the cycle of eternally trying to get dragons to value me, but with no luck? What if Emer loses faith in me? What will the future bring for me?*

The pitter-patter of talons behind him caught his attention. "Emer," he growled. "I told you, I need alone time. Can you go down and see—"

A hard object slammed down on his head. Saphir collapsed to the cool stone beneath him. Everything went black.

* * * * *

Emer sat, leaning against the walls of the cave.

I didn't mean to make him mad, Emer thought. *He just—I wish he'd stop worrying about that. He'll find his element. He'll be happy then.*

The door creaked open. "Saphir? Is that you? I'm sorry!" she said, then looked down.

Paris entered the room. She looked confused. "What are you sorry for Saphir about?"

"Oh, um, it's nothing," Emer said. "Have you seen him anywhere?"

"You unintentionally got him upset about his element again, didn't you?" Paris said, crossing her arms.

Emer shrugged, blowing a spark of fire out of her mouth. "Yeah."

"I saw him go to the usual place he goes whenever he gets upset."

"Where's that?"

"He hasn't told you about it? He has a hiding spot on the roof of the Bluescale cave. It's where he goes to relax when he's stressed. He climbs up a hidden staircase to get there. It's hidden by a small door."

"Got it. I'm going to go see him. I'll be right back," Emer said, walking toward the door.

"What should I do in the meantime?"

"Battle training." Emer rushed out the door. She walked down the hallways, searching for a small door. *Found it!* she thought, pushing open the door. She climbed up the stairs and saw an open hole in the roof. She leaped up, grabbed the edges, and pulled herself up.

"Saphir! I'm sorry I made you upset! Are you feeling any—" she said, her voice echoing back to her.

Saphir was not there.

Where did he go? she wondered, glancing around. *He couldn't have gone somewhere else, could he? But Paris said she saw him come up here. She wouldn't lie about something like that, would she?*

Something caught her eye.

A footprint.

A dirty, red footprint.

She eyed the ground, her heart beating fast. *Dirty, red footprints everywhere,* she thought, following them. They stopped at the edge. *These have not been here before when I've flown over the Bluescale cave.* She poked the print. A little blood droplet clung to her talon. *They're fresh.* The wind whistled by her face. A piece of paper drifted into the air. Emer lunged forward and grabbed the lone piece of paper. She gasped as she saw it.

Saphir's scribbles on a piece of paper and fresh Blood-claw prints everywhere. She leaped off the edge of the cliff, spreading her wings and speeding over the Black Hills beneath her.

It all connects.

The Bloodclaws came and kidnapped Saphir. He's in danger.

He could die.

CHAPTER 13

OBSIDIAN

Saphir blinked his eyes against the darkness. His head throbbed. *Ow.* He grimaced, reaching for it. His claw didn't move. The clinking sound of metal filled his ears.

What the—? He pulled his right forearm forward. Metal clinked again. *I must be chained to a wall,* he thought, swishing his tail; he felt the cool stone ground beneath him. *I must be suspended from the wall. Only my tail is touching the ground.*

What is going on? Where am I? He yanked on the chains, but to no avail. He looked around the dark cave. *I wish Dralerians in dragon form could see in the dark. It would really help me out right now.*

CLICK. CLACK. CLICK. CLACK. The sound of dragon talons echoed around the cave. A quiet, cruel chuckle filled his ears.

"You have regained consciousness, I see," a deep voice purred.

"Demonheart! Is that you? Let me go!" Saphir yelled into the darkness.

"Now prepare for the worst time in your life," the voice roared. "As you have to choose to bow to me . . . or die!"

Saphir's heart pounded in his chest. He gulped. *Who is this dragon? Is it just Demonheart torturing me?*

A torch suddenly burst alive with fire right next to him. His eyes beheld the monstrosity of the dragon in front of him.

The black dragon had spikes and horns that were as smooth and dark as obsidian. It wore a silver necklace with an abnormally large black gemstone, and its mouth was set in a wicked grin. The beast's red-and-black eyes stared straight at Saphir.

This is not Demonheart.

The dragon's grin turned to a frown. "Who are you?" it spat.

"I am Saphir of the Gemstone Warriors!" Saphir yelled, hiding any fear in his voice.

"Saphir? You're a male!" the dragon said, striding over to Saphir. "I sent those Bloodclaws to get Emer, a female! Oh, those numbskulls," he hissed, looking over Saphir. "Although it's not as if you won't be of use to me." The dragon tapped Saphir's light-blue sapphire.

Saphir growled, "Who are you? What do you want with Emer and me?"

"I am Obsidian, faithful and equal ruler with Demonheart of the Bloodclaws," Obsidian purred, lashing his jet-black tail. "You are here because of a stupid mistake. I intended on capturing Emer, but . . . hmm . . ."

Saphir glared at Obsidian. "What are you going to use Emer and me—?"

"You're bait!" Obsidian yelled. "Do you Bluescales not know to stay quiet when one is thinking? I'll keep you here as bait so Emer will come and try to rescue you. When Emer comes, I'll defeat her and use her powers for my own needs." Obsidian paused, then grinned. "Or you could tell me where Emer is right now. Come to think of it, you're a Dralerian as well. I could use Emer's and your powers for myself."

"I refuse to tell you where Emer is and give my powers to you!"

"Tell me where Emer is," Obsidian growled. "Or you'll have to give me your power right now. Either one. I'll be kind and let you choose for the moment."

"What if I don't do either?"

Obsidian chuckled and then lunged at Saphir, swiping his claw at Saphir's throat. Saphir shut his eyes and clenched his jaw, waiting for the strike. He opened his eyes. The talon was inches away from his throat.

"If you do not do what I say," Obsidian said, "I will cut your throat. I will rip out your gemstone and let your blood soak into the stone beneath me. I will let you suffer until you bow to me. I will make you regret not telling or giving me anything."

The gruesome images flashed in his mind. Saphir shook his head and pulled at the chains. *I either tell him where Emer is and get her tortured or, worse, killed; or I could bow to him and get tortured or killed; or I do neither and get myself killed. No matter what I choose, I lose.*

"Tied up about your decision, Bluescale? Let's make it a little faster. You have ten seconds to decide what you do! Ten . . . nine . . . eight . . ."

What do I do?

"Seven . . . six . . ."

BAM! BAM! BAM! The stone door beside him shook. *What is that?*

"Five . . . four . . . three . . ."

The door smashed to pieces. A dragon charged into the room.

"Emer!" Saphir yelled.

"Saphir!" Emer looked up at Saphir where he was chained to the wall.

"Ah, a happy reunion," Obsidian purred. "All to my advantage! Emer, you're supposed to be up there instead of him."

"Who are you?" she roared, smoke rising out of her nose.

"I'm Obsidian, your newest enemy and your worst nightmare." He snickered, holding out his talons. Suddenly, black-and-red fire flared to life in the palms of his claws.

What the—?! How is he doing that?! Saphir thought. He glanced at Emer. Her eyes were wide, and her claws were scratching marks onto the stone. *She's never seen this power before*, he thought, his heart beating fast in his chest.

Obsidian held out his talon, and the black fire flew at Emer. Emer leaped out of the way. She blasted green fire at him. He leaned out of the way and lunged at Emer. They grappled claws, then slashed at one another's scales. They tumbled back, blood dripping from the cuts. Emer lunged forward, ramming Obsidian in the side. He charged at her, scraping his talons across her face.

Emer! Saphir thought. He yanked at his chains. *No use! If only I had an element. I could stop this if I did.*

Obsidian charged at Emer, his black horns smashing into her side. She recoiled, wincing, then charged forward, jaws snapping down on his scales.

No, Saphir thought. *It doesn't matter that I don't have an element. What matters is that I save my friend.*

Obsidian roared, holding out his talons. Fire spurred to life. He spun around, the black flame circling around him. Emer leaned back, then breathed a torrent of flames at Obsidian.

But how do I get out? Saphir ran through every training method he had learned. *Claw swipes, claw jabs, wing extensions, tail swipes . . .*

Obsidian dodged Emer's flame. He shot a blast of fire at Emer. She dodged. Another blast of flame. Dodged again.

Tail. The tail! I can break the chains with the gemstones on my tail! Saphir swung his tail behind him. It hit one of the chains. SNAP! The chain broke into pieces. Saphir fell to the ground.

Obsidian blasted another round of fire. Emer dodged the attack. Almost. The flame hit her lower chest plates, and the force of the attack shoved her against a nearby wall. SLAM! She crumpled to the ground.

"EMER!" Saphir yelled. He swung his tail at the other chain. It snapped apart.

Obsidian approached Emer, each footstep clicking against the ground. "Heh heh heh. Looks like I could bring you down." He laughed, sharp teeth glinting in his cruel smile.

I can save her. I can stop the attack, Saphir thought, dashing over to his friend.

"Emer, we could make all this simple now," Obsidian growled, black-and-red eyes staring at her. "You could join me. All your struggles in life will disappear. All the stupid humans who don't think you're good enough will be avenged if you side with me. You know I don't want you dead; I just want your power. Join me, and you will be free from all your problems." He grinned, teeth flashing in the torchlight.

Emer stared up at him a minute, shock in her eyes. She winced in pain. "Ergh . . . I would rather die and be a noble warrior than side with the likes of you," she growled, placing a claw on the ground. It wobbled, and the cuts bled down her arm.

"All right, then," he said, raising his right forearm. "But you know everything could have been different."

I can save her, Saphir thought, bolting across the floor faster than before. *Because I've learned . . .*

Emer wobbled up on her talons. Obsidian started bringing down his claws.

It's not about what others want you to have . . .

Emer looked at Obsidian's incoming talon.

It's not about the flaws, or what you want to have . . .

Obsidian's grin grew wider. His eyes grew wide.

It's about what you do have, and how you use it for others . . .

Saphir leaped in front of Emer.

Thank you, Emer, for showing me this . . .

Saphir shut his eyes.

THUD! Saphir opened his eyes. Obsidian stumbled back, yelling and holding his talon.

What the—?

"Saphir! Look!" Emer said.

Saphir looked around him. A bluish, spherical sheen surrounded him and Emer. He touched it with his right claw; it was solid.

I have found my element.

Saphir smiled. He had found it. Yet now he realized he was perfect even without it. He watched as the force field around him disappeared.

"You," Obsidian snarled, black-and-red eyes staring straight into Saphir's soul. "How could you . . . how could you?!" Obsidian lunged forward, claws swiping through the air.

Saphir felt his heart leap inside him, but he stayed calm. He watched Obsidian. He waited. Obsidian grew closer. Saphir swept his talon at Obsidian. It sliced across Obsidian's left eye. Blood spurted from the wound.

"AAAAARGH!" Obsidian screamed, falling to the ground. He clenched his eye. His foretalons were covered in blood. His necklace fell off.

But the black gemstone stayed on his chest.

Does that mean . . . ?

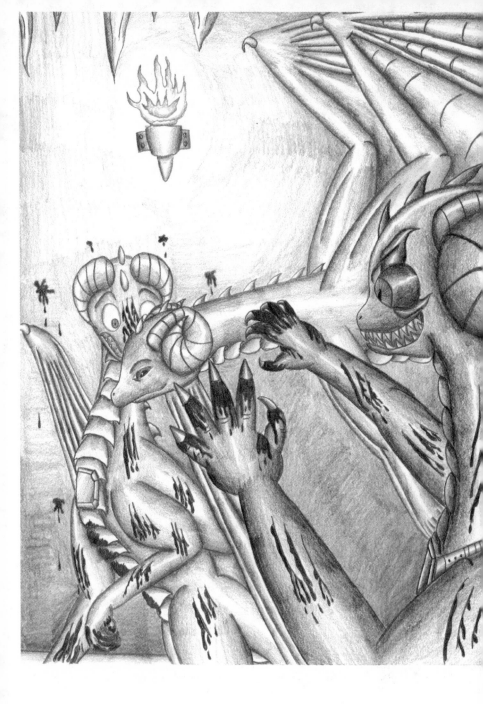

138

"HISSSS!" Obsidian's tail hit a sheet of damaged wood. It toppled over.

"The Dark Energy Crystal!" Saphir exclaimed. It sat on an ornate pedestal in front of him. He dashed forward. He would take back the Crystal. He would stop Obsidian. He would be a hero to the Bluescales.

"Saphir! Stop!" Emer yelled, getting up. She wobbled slightly. Blood dripped down the cuts on her body.

"Why? I could take it from Demonheart and Obsidian's very own talons now! I could save the Bluescales!"

"We don't have any gloves," Emer said. "We don't have anything to protect us from the power of this Crystal."

Saphir looked at Emer, then at the Crystal. *She's right. We can't take it. We have nothing with us to protect us. And there's nothing in this cave to protect us. What rotten luck!*

The sound of growly laughter filled his ears. Obsidian looked at them. His eye was smeared with blood.

"Fools," Obsidian muttered. "FOOLS! To beat your master! To make me bleed! I will make you pay . . . I WILL make you KNEEL to ME!"

"Run," Emer said, shoving Saphir out of Obsidian's cave.

Saphir stood in the hallway. "No! We're trapped in here!"

"No, we're not," Emer said. "I know the way out." She dashed down a hallway, wobbling on her injured forearm. Saphir followed. Their talons echoed in the small, narrow hallway. She dashed down a hallway to the right, then one to the left. Right, left, and right again. Saphir followed, scanning their surroundings for Bloodclaws.

Emer dashed down another hallway. Moonlight shone on the ground. She leaped up through a hole, taking to the air. Saphir leaped, flapping his wings. He felt heavy and tired as he took to the sky.

The wind pushed them higher. Saphir kept flying. *I can't rest*, he thought. *I can't fold my wings or collapse onto the ground, or else he will catch me. He will kill me.*

I have to fly for my life.

CHAPTER 14

CALM BEFORE THE STORM

Emer flapped her wings. The wind whistled in her face. Her forearms and wings ached. *We're almost there. We're almost there.*

"There it is!" Emer said. She looked at the Flight Ledge. *I feel as if I haven't seen it in so long,* Emer thought, breathing a sigh of relief. *We're almost home.* She dived toward the rocky ledge. She spread her wings, slowed, and tumbled onto the Flight Ledge, exhausted. At last, she exhaled.

"Emer?" a voice asked. There was a soft thud on the ground. Saphir strode over to her.

"Saphir," Emer said, looking up at him. She sat up slowly because her head was spinning. "You were brave in there."

"Me? Brave? I think you're mistaken," he said. "You were the one who battled Obsidian head-on. He was a crazy-minded freak, I'll tell you that."

"Yeah," Emer said, then winced, grabbing her right forearm. Blood oozed down the long cut on her arm.

"Oh, dear," he said. He reached out with his right foreclaw and grabbed her right foretalon. "I should try to heal you like we did four weeks ago. Remember?"

I remember, she thought. *That has been the one and only time it's worked. Since then, we've tried to heal ourselves and other dragons without gemstones, but it hasn't worked.* "Saphir, it hasn't happened in four weeks," she said. "I don't think it will now."

"I also didn't think I'd get my element," he said, "but I did."

Suddenly, the sapphire on his gemstone flashed. Emer watched as her emerald started glowing. She watched as light flooded into the cut not just on her right forearm but also into the cuts, burns, and bruises all over her body. Emer shut her eyes, but the light still entered them.

In a moment, the light died away. Emer looked at her scales. The cuts, burns, and bruises were gone.

"Why did it work now and not all the times earlier?" Emer wondered aloud, sliding her talons over her smooth blue scales.

"Well, the two times it's worked have been when we were in intense battles and we were looking after one another. The other times we've tried it and failed have been when we missed the battle or tried to heal other dragons without gemstones," Saphir said.

"You think that the only way our gemstone healing power works is when two or more Dralerians have battled together and helped one another out?"

"Yeah."

"Ah," Emer said. "And you found your element!" Emer exclaimed, grinning from horn to horn. "I told you that you would!" She poked him with her talon.

He grinned and poked her back. "Part of me still feels as if something is missing," he said, "but I'm happy and relieved. But when Obsidian was going to attack you, I realized I was wrong about the whole 'if I don't have an element, I'm useless' thing."

Emer shrugged. "It's okay. We all make mistakes."

"I think you should use that for yourself," Saphir continued. "I thought that if I didn't have an element, I was useless. You seem to think that if you don't change yourself to fit in with other girls your age, your human life isn't worth anything."

"That's what my mother told me," Emer said, lashing her tail.

"That's how some people think. They want you to change. They want you to fit their criteria, and they believe you'll never fit in unless you do. However, your true friends in life will appreciate you for who you are."

"And those people are . . . ?" Emer asked with a smirk.

"Oh, come on, now! Gabby likes you because you're a kind, open friend to her who gives her advice. Paris likes you because you laugh at her jokes and joke around with her. And I . . ."

"You like to see how I react when you annoy me with your schedules?" Emer smirked, raising an eye ridge.

"No, no, not the schedule stuff. I . . . I think you're perfect just the way you are," Saphir murmured, moving his right foreclaw onto her shoulder.

Emer stared into his kind, green eyes. She felt the scales on her face grow hot, and she scratched the scales behind her horns. "Well, thanks," she said quietly. "Anyway," she added, watching as Saphir moved his talon away from her, "about Obsidian. He's a threat. He would be a Rank 4 on the Bloodclaw Rank Chart at the least."

"He's definitely as powerful as Demonheart," Saphir agreed. "I think that's because he's a Dralerian."

"What? What makes you think that?"

"He was wearing a necklace when I met him," Saphir explained. "When I hit his eye and he rolled on the ground, his necklace came off, but not the gemstone. It stayed on his chest."

"I thought there were only supposed to be four in existence," Emer said. "You know, because of the Foretelling."

"But you were friends with Iridigrarr," Saphir said. "Technically, that would make it five in existence. Six, if you count Obsidian. Unless . . ."

"Unless?"

"Are you sure Iridigrarr died? Are you absolutely positive his heart stopped beating?"

Emer's eyes widened, then narrowed. Smoke billowed out of her nose. "Are you accusing my deceased companion of being the monstrous, murderous beast we just encountered?"

"I'm not accusing, just hypothesizing," Saphir said.

"Saphir, I can tell you quite clearly that the dragon we just encountered is not Iridigrarr!" Emer yelled. "Iridigrarr was a kind, wonderful dragon with red scales, not a terrifying black monstrosity! I watched my friend die in a pool of his own blood. I heard him breathe his very last breath. For you to have the audacity to accuse him of such a—"

"I was only wondering because he looks like a Bluescale and has advanced elemental powers!" Saphir stated, voice raised. "Wasn't Iridigrarr a Bluescale? Didn't Iridigrarr have advanced elemental powers?"

"Yes, but that is not him!" Emer yelled. "Iridigrarr would never do such a thing! He would never kill an innocent dragon!"

"Unless he happened to have gotten power from the Dark Energy Crystal."

"He was dead, Saphir! Dead! Besides, if Iridigrarr were the evil beast we ran into, he wouldn't know so much about our school life! Iridigrarr was, for some unknown reason, not able to transform from human to dragon with his gemstone! Whoever that dragon is knows about our life outside of his dragon form!"

"Okay, okay," Saphir said. "It's not Iridigrarr risen from the dead. We've determined that."

"I know it's not," Emer huffed. "Since we've crossed that unlikely suspect off our list, who's left?"

"Since Obsidian knows about our personal lives, it's got to be someone we know in our human forms as well," Saphir pondered. "Perhaps its someone in our school."

"Yeah, that would make sense," Emer said, walking inside the Bluescale cave. "I did find that notebook with the drawing of the Dark Energy Crystal in it. I still don't know who it belongs to, though. There was no name written on the inside."

"Are you sure it was the Dark Energy Crystal?" Saphir asked, following her. "You know, some kids do draw things that look like some of the stuff you see here."

"I'm positive," she said. "I've seen that Crystal my whole life. I know exactly what it looks like. I've also seen every kid's drawing style in Red Raven Middle School. Half the kids don't draw, a quarter of the kids draw real-life objects, and the other quarter draw characters from cartoons. Although . . ."

"What?"

"I haven't seen George's art style yet or what he likes to draw," Emer said. "He's the one kid I don't know a lot about yet in our school."

"Wait," Saphir said, eyes wide. "Do you still have the notebook with you?"

"Yeah. Why?"

"George has been looking for something since you've been suspended from school. Do you think what he's looking for is the notebook?"

"Have you asked him what he's looking for?" Emer asked.

"No, and I'm pretty sure that if I did, he wouldn't tell me," Saphir said.

You know, George has been different from all the other kids at the school I've seen, Emer thought. *He gives off that fire-like feeling, and he's strangely quiet around other kids. Come to think of it, he was hesitant to shake my hand when I met him, as if he didn't know what I was doing.* "Saphir," Emer said, "do you think—?"

"There you are!" a voice exclaimed. Emer looked down. Paris was walking toward them. "You were gone for so long! You guys know it's, like, one in the morning, right?"

"One in the morning! I've got to get back home," Saphir said.

"Same," Paris agreed.

"Oh. I have to stay here," Emer said. "The Council is having a meeting in two hours, and I have to alert them about the new threat. Plus, my mom will be at the hospital until noon, and I'm suspended from school."

"What new danger?" Paris demanded. "And how will you stay awake here? You've had no sleep!"

"I slept all day before I came here," Emer said.

"Paris, how about we head home?" Saphir asked, crouching down. "If we don't get back soon, our mothers will come looking for us."

"True," Paris said, climbing up on Saphir's back. "But you have to explain to me what the new danger is and why you two were gone so long."

"I will," Saphir said. "We'll be headed off now." He ran down the hallway, toward the Flight Ledge.

"Bye! Stay safe! Take the long way home!" Emer yelled, watching as her friends took off into the night sky.

* * * * *

"CAW! CAW! CAW!"

Iridigrarr held out his right foretalon, and the crow hopped up. Iridigrarr's eye stung as if there were fire burning into it.

"Are you worried about me, my little fluffy-puff?" Iridi-grarr purred, smiling at the bundle of black feathers. "Well, you can blame this all on EMER AND HER STUPID BOY-FRIEND, SAPHIR!" he roared.

"CAAAAW!" The crow's head bounced up and down.

"See? You agree with me! That's why you're my best friend!"

The click-clack of talons echoed from out in the hallway. *The Bloodclaws are coming.* Iridigrarr tapped his garnet gemstone. His color changed from red to black. *The Blood-claws cannot know I'm Iridigrarr,* he thought. *They must know me as Obsidian.*

"Aku arnar eisser?" Several Bloodclaws peeked into his room.

"Come in," Iridigrarr hissed. His crow hopped onto his shoulder. *I hate having to use all these Bloodclaws. They mess things up half the time. This time, however, I have no other option.*

The Bloodclaws stalked into the cave, looking about.

"I have a demand for you," Iridigrarr said.

"Issir anr nar HISS!" one of the Bloodclaws said.

"No. It's not slicing a crow's throat! Why would you even say that?"

"Hissir," another Bloodclaw said.

"What I need you to do is sneak into the Bluescale caves via the Bloodclaw Tunnel System," Iridigrarr said. "Those that succeed will get scraps for a week. Those that do not . . ."

"Arkarr nunu?"

"You all will be crow food!" Iridigrarr roared. "Now go! Fulfill my plan! Kill all in sight!"

The Bloodclaws fled from the cave, claws scraping the stone ground in the hallway.

"Go perch over there," Iridigrarr said. The crow flew over to Iridigrarr's throne.

Iridigrarr walked out of his cave, his footsteps hurried, yet powerful. *I know Demonheart would ridicule me for my plan. He would mock me because of the high risk. He would beat me for my foolishness.*

However, he wouldn't know I was prepared.

I was prepared for Emer's possible escape. I found the basis for a plan and created an even better one. Those filthy Bloodclaws are doing their part. I will head out to fulfill my part of the plan.

He walked down the hallway toward the end of the cave glowing with light.

Emer, you may think all the Chosen Ones are strong and mighty, but that's not the case. You have a weak link who has revealed much about you to me. I will use that all to my advantage.

One of the Chosen Ones' powers will be mine.

He leaped out of the cave and spread his ebony wings, taking to the skies.

The pieces of my plan are all falling into place.

Emer, you may think you'll win, but that's not the case.

I will be the victor in this war.

CHAPTER 15

THE BLOODCLAWS
ARE COMING

I think you'll be able to fight again.

The words echoed in Skye's mind. *That Chosen One from the Foretelling, that girl . . . what was her name? Paris? Her words have been stuck in my head.*

"Uh, Skye? That is your name, right?" a voice asked.

"Huh? Oh, oh yes," Skye said, looking at the small Pinescale sitting by him. "I was just thinking about something, that's all."

"Cool."

Skye adjusted the large wooden pencil in his grip. It scratched against the paper, then slipped out of his talons.

"Argh! Why is this so hard?" he exclaimed, thudding his new, titanium forearm against the ground.

"Well, it takes time to learn how to do something with a part of your body you've never used," Scalene said. "You were left-clawed?"

"Yeah," he said. *I don't know what I think of this new dragon*, Skye thought. *I know that Vladmir wanted us to get to know other injured dragons recovering in these caves, but I just want to be alone right now.*

"Wait. Wait one minute!" Scalene dashed over on her two back legs and looked at Skye's new forearm. "Are you the Bluescale that survived that sneak Bloodclaw attack?"

"Oh . . . yeah," he said, scratching the scales behind his horns.

"Seriously, you were so brave!" Scalene cheered. "The fact that you pulled through and survived that horrid attack was awesome! You are a super-strong dragon to survive the Backward-Scale battle strategy!"

"The what?" Skye asked.

"The Backward-Scale battle strategy is a strategy that dragons use in attacks. They stage from one to several big, catastrophic attacks that distract everyone, but underneath, they're doing something even more sinister," Scalene explained.

"How do you know that my attack was a Backward-Scale strategy?"

"When I was lying on the fur in my room, I overheard Vladmir talking with another Bluescale about how you were injured in the big Bloodclaw attack that distracted everyone. That's a type of Backward-Scale strategy."

"Oh," Skye said. "That's good to know, I guess."

"Yeah. There was another attack that happened tonight, actually," Scalene said.

"What? What happened?"

"According to what I heard from Vladmir's conversation, Saphir was kidnapped tonight by the Bloodclaws. Thankfully, Emer was able to rescue him."

Skye began connecting the dots. *First the Bloodclaws steal the Dark Energy Crystal, then Saphir gets kidnapped . . . of course, the Council will hear about this.*

Wait.

If Majesty calls an emergency meeting for the Council, and all dragons go in to listen . . .

"Scalene! We're all in danger!" Skye exclaimed. He stumbled up onto his forearms.

"What do you mean we're in danger?"

"Demonheart is pulling a Backward-Scale battle strategy on us now! He distracted all the dragons with the kidnapping of Saphir, so now Bloodclaws can sneak into the cave! I have to telecommunicate to Emer!"

He let his mind relax and contacted her mind. "Emer! Are you there?"

"Skye? Is that you?" Emer's voice asked in his mind.

"Yes! I need you, Majesty, Knifeclaw, and any guards to join me in the Treasure Tunnels! There's going to be another Bloodclaw attack!" Skye telecommunicated to her.

"What? How are you sure of this?"

"Someone just told me about something called the Backward-Scale battle strategy!"

"By the scales and tail of the Greatwing, you're right! Meet you down in the Treasure Tunnels. Stay safe." Emer's voice faded from his mind.

"Great. I have backup," Skye said. He hobbled over to the door of his room and pushed it open.

"Where are you going? You have to stay and rest!" Scalene demanded, fluttering up into the air.

"I'm going to go defeat those Bloodclaws barging in here. Care to join me? You're the dragon a Bloodclaw tried to eat, correct?"

Scalene hovered in place. "Count me in." She fluttered over next to him.

Bloodclaws, Skye thought, walking down the purple-lit hallway. *You may have defeated my father, and you may have wounded me. But I assure you, this time, I will come out victorious.*

* * * * *

As Skye hid behind a rock, the dim light in the cave glimmered off his scales.

"Are you sure your estimation was correct?" Emer asked, gripping the rock beside him.

"Positive. I have a keen intuition about these things," he said, glancing around. Guards were hidden everywhere within the tunnels.

"You know, his intuition wouldn't have known about it without my help," Scalene said, standing beside Skye.

"You two figured this out together?"

Scalene nodded.

I do hope my intuition was right, Skye thought. *If I interrupted an important meeting of the Council for a mistake . . .* Skye shuddered. He couldn't be wrong.

"Please, brother, I beg that you keep yourself safe," Stonehorn said, worry in his voice.

Skye looked at him. *I still don't understand why Emer telecommunicated to him to come and join us. He doesn't fight.* "Stonehorn, I will stay safe. I am almost positive we will emerge victorious in this sneak Bloodclaw attack."

"But what about your . . . uh . . . forearm?" Stonehorn asked.

A poof of smoke drifted out of Skye's nostrils. "Trust me. I'll be fine."

"Okay. But I'm right here if anything goes wrong. I'm a Cavedweller, you know. I can treat wounded dragons and stuff."

"Shhh!" Scalene hissed. The frills on the side of her head spread out, twitching. "I heard something."

"I didn't hear anything," Stonehorn said.

"But she might have," Skye said.

"Everyone, just shut your mouths and listen," Emer ordered.

Skye shut his mouth. He listened to the eerie silence that filled the Treasure Tunnels. *This is unnerving,* Skye thought, eyes scanning his surroundings. *But I will stay here and stand strong. I must be brave. I must avenge my father.*

CLICK. CLACK. CLICK. CLACK. A chill swept over Skye's scales. Skye glanced over the rock. His heart thudded against his chest. Three pairs of glowing yellow eyes shone through the darkness in the Mining Tunnel.

"Is that . . . ?" Stonehorn asked.

"It is." Skye breathed. He felt his stomach twist inside him. *I cannot be nervous. I can do this!*

"Akarr ner ner herr," one of the Bloodclaws growled, entering the Treasure Tunnel.

"Far far ner ner," another one growled.

"On my word," Emer telecommunicated to Skye. He glanced around. All the other guards were staring at Emer. *She's telecommunicating with everyone,* Skye thought. *She truly is one of the best telecommunicators in this cave.*

"One . . . two . . ."

"Three!" Emer yelled.

Skye leaped out from behind his rock. He charged at a Bloodclaw, wobbling on his artificial forearm. It looked at him, then hissed.

"Hiss at this!" Skye yelled. He slammed his titanium forearm into the Bloodclaw's head. There was a large CRACK, and blood dripped down the wound. Skye blasted fire at the stunned Bloodclaw.

"AAAREARGH!" it howled as it collapsed to the ground, covered in flames.

Skye looked over. He saw Scalene tackling another Bloodclaw, shredding its scales with her small talons. She dodged its every attack and breathed a gust of flame at the beast.

"HISSSS," the Bloodclaw growled, lunging forward. Scalene dodged the attack and swiped her talons across its neck. It fell to the ground, dead.

There was a THUD. Skye looked over. The third and final Bloodclaw fell to the ground. Emer and several guards stood around it.

Skye looked back toward the rock they had hidden behind. Stonehorn's head poked up from behind the rock. His eyes were wide, and the tips of his wings were shaking.

Stonehorn, it's a good thing you're a Cavedweller, Skye thought. *You would never be able to handle the stuff I have had to handle.* Skye watched Stonehorn walk out from behind the rock. *But maybe our differences are valuable . . . We both help the colony in different ways. I know Father may have ridiculed you for your role in this cave, but I don't know if he had ever seen how hard you work.*

A blast of fire caught his attention. Majesty strode into the cave, his head and large horns held high. His eyes glanced from Skye to Emer to the damage around them.

Knifeclaw prowled into the tunnels as well. He looked around, raising his eye ridges. "Who knew this attack would take place? Who figured it out?"

"Whoever did has saved us all and shall be declared a hero," Majesty declared.

"Those two did it," Emer said. Her talon pointed at Scalene and Skye.

Skye looked at her talon, then up at the towering figures of Majesty and Knifeclaw.

"You two figured it out?" Knifeclaw growled.

"Hey!" Scalene hissed. "I may be small, but I'm ferocious! I took down that Bloodclaw with my bare talons and no help at all!" The purple, scaly crest on her head was raised, and her eyes narrowed.

"Yes, they did figure it out," Stonehorn said. "They really did."

Majesty eyed Skye. He glanced over at Scalene. "You

two . . . you look different from all other dragons here, yet you figured it out."

Skye's heart sank. *Majesty doesn't believe it, does he?*

"That is why this is even more exceptional!" Majesty cheered. "Despite your differences, you saved our tribe from yet another attack! You all are heroes!"

The guards all cheered. Stonehorn ran up to his brother. "Skye! You did it! I shouldn't have doubted you, really. I was just nervous, especially after . . ."

"It's all right," Skye said, grinning. "I wasn't sure I could do it, either."

"But you did. Everyone is cheering for you. You're a hero."

Skye's eyes widened. He looked at the dragons around him.

All these dragons are cheering for me, he thought, the smile on his face growing. *I may be injured for life, but I still did it. I figured out the attack. I attacked the invaders. I won. Just because I'm different doesn't mean I can't help protect anymore. I'm a hero.*

Paris, you were right. I fought again. And I won.

* * * * *

Emer watched the happy scene before her.

A dragon who days ago was on the verge of death is now a hero. He's happy, she thought. *Another dragon, the one I saved, has proved she's still a fighter, no matter her size.*

It looks like it's a happy ending for everyone. Good thing they figured out what that attack was: the Backward-Scale battle strategy. If not for that, we'd never have known about this attack coming. Wait . . .

Emer's mind flashed back to Saphir's kidnapping. She thought about her fight with Obsidian, how Saphir had discovered his element, and how they escaped before Obsidian could attack them again.

Obsidian knew. Obsidian knew that, after Saphir and I escaped, we'd tell the Council about him. He knew that I'd be busy with the Council while he sent Bloodclaws to attack us and that I would be even busier attacking the incoming Bloodclaws. What if . . .

What if this attack was also a distraction?

Oh, snake fangs!

"I've got to go!" Emer yelled. She charged past the crowd of dragons up the entryway to the Treasure Tunnels. She ran, her claws thudding against the ground.

I can't believe it! I fell right into Obsidian's talons! she scolded herself. *I never saw it coming! Argh!*

If he does what I think he'll do . . . if this attack was purely meant for distraction . . . I'll know what he really wanted.

He wanted me to be busy and out of the way.

He wants to hurt my friends without my being there to stop him.

Well, that's not going to be the case, Emer thought, leaping off the Flight Ledge into the sky. *I'm on my way.*

CHAPTER 16

THE STORM IS HERE

Ah . . . yesterday was such a good day!

Gabby opened her locker door, grinning from ear to ear. *George was so kind to me yesterday. He bought me the best kind of fro-yo, and we sat at a table and ate together. When he walked me home, he held my hand.* Gabby sighed, feeling her cheeks grow warm. *He is the best person I've ever met!*

"Hello, Gabby," a voice said behind her.

"EEEP! Oh, I mean, hi, George!" Gabby grinned, facing her beloved one.

"I had such a wonderful time with you last night," George said, grabbing her hands. "You were so beautiful in the glow of the fluorescent lighting, I could hardly speak! Your hair flows down your shoulders like a caramel waterfall, and your dark green eyes glitter like peridot!"

Gabby's face grew red. Her heart beat in her chest. "Thanks." She grinned and looked up at him. *It looks like there's cover-up on part of his left eye . . .*

"Gabby, you'll love this new fro-yo place I found. It's not that far from school, and they serve fifty flavors. Fifty! We should head out there."

"Yeah! Let's go right away after school!" Gabby said.

George looked at her, the smile disappearing from his face. "I meant right now."

Gabby paused. She felt her excitement slip away. "Now? But it's school, and we need to head to class. I'd love to go after class, but not now. Okay?" She shut her locker door and started walking.

He gripped her shoulder. "We're going now," George demanded, his warm, comforting voice suddenly harsh and cold. Gabby shivered. He wrapped his arm around her shoulders and walked down the hallway. Butterflies of fear fluttered in Gabby's stomach.

What is George doing? Gabby thought, glancing around. *This isn't right. Why is he doing this? Is he going to hurt me?*

Wait, she thought, smiling weakly. *He loves me. I love him. He would never do anything to get me in trouble or hurt me.*

Right?

* * * * *

"Raider, you have to listen to me."

Raider sighed. *Why must she argue about this again?* "Paris, you must know that what I'm saying is the truth. Wizarding World is a much better book series than Fire and Flame."

"Lies! All lies!" Paris protested. "Fire and Flame is so much better than Wizarding World!"

"Really? What makes it better?"

"My favorite book series has lots of dragons in it!"

"So does Wizarding World!"

"Too much magic, not enough dragons!"

"Oh, really?"

"Yeah! If Gabby were here, she'd agree with me!" Paris said, crossing her arms and sticking her nose in the air.

"Actually, I don't think Gabby likes either of those series," Raider said, looking back at Gabby's desk. "Speaking of Gabby, where is she?"

"Huh," Paris said. "I don't know. Do you think she's sick or had an appointment of some kind?"

"She would have texted us," Raider said, looking back at Paris. "You don't think something's wrong, do you?"

"Hmm, let me think," Paris said, putting her hand on her chin. "Let's see, last we heard from her, she was heading out with George." She paused. "She was heading out with George. I knew that numbskull would hurt her!" Paris exclaimed, pounding her hands on her desk.

"Paris, we don't know that," Raider whispered, grabbing her hands and pressing them to her desk. "She could have just gotten sick."

"Really? Is that what your mind is telling you?"

Raider thought it over. *It is true that she would text us,* he thought, *and with George . . .*

"You're right," Raider said.

"Yes! We should go find her now! I bet George did something to harm her."

"How can we leave class?" Raider asked. "Besides, our class is with Mr. Wellington. How will he react if he sees us leaving?"

"He won't react, because we're leaving now," Paris said, leaping up from her desk. She dashed out of the room.

"Hey! Wait up!" Raider said, chasing after her. He ran out of the room and stopped next to her by a bunch of lockers.

"Let's look for her, okay?" Paris said.

"Stealthily," Raider said.

"All right, we'll look for her stealthily."

* * * * *

BRRRRRINNNNG! The bell for class rang.

Bella sneaked along the sides of the hallway. She glanced around from the sides of lockers, scanning the hallway.

Where is that kid? she thought, looking around the empty hallways. *George isn't in class. He's not in any of the other rooms in this building . . . where is he?*

She pulled the black hood on her sweatshirt farther over her head and walked down the hallway. *Thank goodness I had time to stop at home and grab some dark-colored clothes.*

Bella froze. The squeak-squeak of sneakers echoed in the hallway. *Someone's coming!* Bella hid behind the side of a set of lockers. *Why does this have to be so hard? If only I weren't suspended, it would be so much easier to look for him! Ugh, if only there were an easier way to find George!*

Bella watched as Lucy walked by her. Lucy stopped at a locker and clicked it open.

Wait a minute. Can't she find someone within minutes thanks to social media? I know she doesn't like me! Could I really trust her? Bella thought of her friends. She sighed. *I'd rather trust Lucy for a minute than lose my friends forever.*

"Psst! Psst! Lucy!" Bella whispered.

Lucy glanced around. "Who's there?"

"Come over here! By the lockers!" Bella whispered as Lucy walked over.

"Who are you?" she asked.

Bella pulled the hood off her head. "It's the person you like the least," she said.

"You! What are you doing here, Bella? You're suspended!" Lucy sneered.

"I had to come," Bella whispered. "One of my friends has something I need to retrieve."

"Really? And it couldn't wait until after school?"

"No, it couldn't!" Bella hissed. "I just . . . I need you to . . . do me a favor," Bella choked out.

Lucy laughed. "You need a favor? From me? In your

dreams. You got me suspended for two days and yelled at me over a pencil."

"Please!"

"Maybe," she said, looking at her bright-pink fingernails. "What's in it for me?"

"I'll never talk to you again," Bella said. "I'll never look at you or ask anything from you again, unless a teacher orders it."

"Even if I somehow have your pencil?" Lucy asked.

"Even if you somehow have my pencil."

Lucy looked at Bella. "Fine," she spat. "That deal works for me. What do you need me to do?"

"Go onto your social media. See if anyone has seen George," Bella said.

"Why not just ask your friend Gabby? Or maybe you didn't know that they're the school's hottest new couple?" Lucy muttered, clicking on her phone.

"Hot new couple?!" Bella exclaimed. "Well, no, George just has something I need for my homework, so . . ."

"You need it now." Lucy typed in something on her phone. DING! DING! DING! The phone made noise after noise.

"They responded that fast?" Bella asked, looking at Lucy's phone.

"They always do," Lucy said. "It looks like your friends were last seen around the hallway with the broken emergency exit."

"You mean the door with an alarm that doesn't go off anymore?"

"That's the one."

"Great! Thanks!" Bella pulled the hood over her head and glanced around the hallway.

"You are really weird, you know that?" Lucy said.

Bella looked back at Lucy. She thought of when her mother had told her to change. She thought of when Lucy had told her she'd never fit in. She thought of when Raider had said that her true friends would appreciate her for who she was.

If I were trying to be normal right now, I'd be at home. I'd probably try to stop associating with the Bluescales. I'd give up my drawings, my books, my love of dragons. I wouldn't be here trying to save my friends from an evil dragon.

Raider was right. I'm perfect just the way I am.

"Well," Bella said, shrugging, "that's just who I am."

Lucy looked at Bella, a perplexed expression on her face. Bella smirked at her and dashed down the hallway.

Watch out, George, Bella thought. *I'm coming.*

* * * * *

"No luck. None at all," Raider said.

"Seriously?" Paris asked. "They weren't hiding in the old storage room?"

"No." Raider sighed. *This is getting frustrating. There's no sign of Gabby or George anywhere.* "Maybe they're not here," Raider said. "Perhaps we should just go back to class."

"Give up? Are you crazy?" Paris asked. "No! I'm not giving up now! Are you positive we've searched the whole building?"

"Yes."

"Then let's look outside."

"Outside?" Raider exclaimed. "We can't go outside now! We've already broken enough school rules!"

"George will have broken more if he does something to hurt Gabby! Is there a door around here so we can sneak out without anyone seeing us?"

"Well, there are the front entryways, but those doors have security guards, so we'd be spotted. There are emergency exits, but we'd surely be heard leaving from one of those." Raider glanced over. "However, there is that one broken exit with an alarm that doesn't work anymore."

"Seriously? That's where George went! I'm sure of it!" Paris said. "Where is this door?"

"Right over there." Raider pointed to a gray metal door near them.

Paris glanced over. "Let's go!" She ran over to the door and pushed it open.

Raider followed her and stepped outside. The wind blasted in his face, taking his breath away. The long strands of prairie grass whipped about under the cloudy gray sky.

Raider looked around. *Any people standing out in the open would be Gabby and George. This school was built on undeveloped land, so there's pretty much nothing else out here.*

"Look! I see something!" Paris said. She pointed out in the field. A blond head stuck out over the brown grass.

"That's George," Raider said. He looked closely and saw another head. "Gabby is with him."

"Let's go!" Paris exclaimed. She ran into the long grass, pushing the stalks out of her way. Raider followed. The grass whipped around him, and the wind howled in his ears.

"Hey! George!" Paris yelled. "Stop! Slow down! We need to talk!"

Raider kept running. He and Paris kept getting closer and closer, but still, George and Gabby did not stop.

"Hey, doofus! Turn around and face us, you coward!" Paris yelled.

George and Gabby stopped in their tracks. George turned, his arm around Gabby's shoulders. Raider slowed, then came to a stop. Paris walked forward.

"What are you two doing out of school?" George asked. "You're missing some very educational classes."

"Same goes for you, bozo," Paris snapped. "What are you doing with our friend?"

"Oh, she and I wanted to go to this new fro-yo place downtown," George said, pulling Gabby even closer. "She wanted to go so badly that I just had to take her there."

Raider looked at Gabby. *There's fear in her eyes. She never wanted to go.*

"Gabby knows how important it is to go to school," Raider said. "She would never skip a class."

"Gabby! If you're scared, tell us! You can defend yourself!" Paris said.

"George, are you sure this can't wait until after class?" Gabby whimpered.

"No! Now let's go!" George snarled.

Raider's eyes widened. *Whoa. That was unexpected.*

George turned around and began to walk away. Gabby looked back at Paris and Raider. Paris nodded.

"George . . . I don't want fro-yo now. I want to go to class with my friends," she said, a sliver of confidence rising in her voice.

"No! We're going!"

"I'm not," Gabby said, lifting George's arm and shoving him away from her.

"What are you doing?" he yelled, grabbing her shoulders. "You're not leaving me! You are staying with me!"

"I don't think I want to anymore."

"Fine. FINE!" He shoved Gabby to the ground.

"That does it!" Paris yelled as she ran toward George. "You can't hurt my friend!"

Raider followed, and George raised his arms in defense.

"I most certainly can," he snarled, raising his hands and folding them into fists. "I've had enough of you three. It's time I teach you a lesson." George lunged forward at Paris. Paris charged at George.

"STOP!"

George stopped. Paris stopped. Gabby stood up. Raider looked back.

A figure in black sweatpants and a black hooded sweatshirt stood a short distance from them. The hood concealed the person's identity.

"Whoever you are, leave us," George barked.

"I don't think so," the person said. She pulled off her hood. Long, brown hair flew back, blowing in the wind.

Bella! Raider thought.

"You want this, George?" she asked. She pulled one of her hands out of her pockets and held up a leather notebook.

George's perfect blue eyes went wide. "How did you find that?"

"None of your business, George," Bella said. Her other hand whipped out of her pocket and hurled something at him.

George's eyes stayed focused on the notebook. He only glanced at the object Bella threw when it was too late.

The gray object hit George in the chest. CRACK!

Something broke in his chest! Raider thought. *But . . . it sounded like glass. Could it be . . . ?*

Suddenly, bright light flashed up from around George. He grew larger, and scales morphed onto his skin. Wings and a tail lashed out, and, finally, a black, cracked gemstone appeared on his chest.

Is it . . . ? It is.

I can't believe it.

A black dragon stood before them. His face was contorted with fury.

"Or," Bella said, "should I say Obsidian? Hello again, you sneaky basilisk."

CHAPTER 17

FIGHTING OBSIDIAN

I figured it out.

I caught him red-clawed.

Bella stared at the scene before her. Raider, Paris, and Gabby stared at George, now Obsidian. Obsidian kept tapping the gemstone on his chest.

"Why won't it work? Why won't it work!" Obsidian yelled.

"Don't you know about Dralerian anatomy?" Bella asked. "A Dralerian, whether human or dragon, always has a gemstone on his or her chest. For humans, it's hidden on the bones in their rib cage. If anything should happen to hurt their gemstone . . ."

"It hurts them," Raider said, backing away from Obsidian.

"Do you mean . . . ?" Paris asked.

"You took away my ability to transform into a human?"

Obsidian roared.

"Precisely," Bella said.

"You . . . you!" Obsidian thundered, stamping his claws on the ground. "You escaped from me when I almost had you in my grasp. Now you've thwarted my plan to kidnap and use the other Chosen Ones! You snake-fanged lizard!" Black fire whirled out of his mouth, covering the ground below in flames. Raider, Paris, and Gabby dashed away, and Bella ran toward her friends.

"Bella!" Raider said, eyes wide. "Our discussion earlier about who Obsidian might be . . . our guesses were right. It was George."

"Yeah," Bella said. "After stopping another Bloodclaw attack and thinking about what we knew, I knew it was him and that he was going to attack, so I retaliated."

"It only took you quite a while to catch on," Obsidian snarled. Smoke billowed out of his nostrils. "I figured you would catch on much sooner, Bella."

"I caught on soon enough with your Backward-Scale strategy!" Bella yelled, staring straight into his black-and-red eyes.

"No, not just that," Obsidian said. "All the other stuff I did beforehand."

"Other stuff?" Raider said.

"Like what?" Paris demanded.

"I was the one who planned the stealing of the Dark Energy Crystal," Obsidian said. "That was my move to get the Bluescales anxious again. Then I scouted out your human forms. It was hard to find where all of you might be, but I found where you four were on my first try. Not only did the four of you stay close together, you gave off a very different vibe from everyone else. Once I knew you in human form, I started working to get you to trust me—and eventually give me your powers. Unfortunately, none of you trusted me except Gabby, who told me everything about you, from small things to big, emotional things I could use against you."

Obsidian smirked. "Bella, you're the strongest one in the group, so I needed to get you out of the way for a while. When I found out you didn't like Lucy, I saw my chance. I destroyed the art display case by tipping it over. When I was sitting next to you at the art table, I stole your pencil and put it next to Lucy. You hated her so much, you thought she did it! Thankfully, that argument got you out of the picture. I was able to use Gabby for all the information I needed, and the other two couldn't do anything about it!"

"You . . . you monster!" Paris yelled. "You diabolical maniac!"

"You're the one that got me suspended?" Bella exclaimed. "You're the one who planned all those attacks?"

"That is evil," Raider said.

"How could you do this to me?" Gabby cried out.

Obsidian's wicked grin turned into a sympathetic frown. "Oh, I'm sorry, Gabby darling, did I hurt your feelings?"

"Yes!"

"I'm deeply sorry. Remember, I'm not an evil dragon to my core, Gabby," Obsidian said, walking toward Gabby. "Deep inside, I have the heart and soul of the George you know and love."

Gabby looked up at Obsidian. Her frowned softened. "You do?"

"Gabby! Don't do this!" Paris yelled. "He's setting you up! It's a trap!"

"Don't listen to her," Obsidian whispered, staring into Gabby's eyes. "Listen to me."

"Obsidian! Get away from her!" Bella yelled, running toward Gabby.

Obsidian's eyes flashed. He leaped off the ground. Gabby jumped back. Obsidian grabbed her with his back talons. Gabby screamed.

"NO!" Bella yelled.

"HA HA HA!" Obsidian cackled. "Sweet, sweet revenge!"

"But . . . but we loved one another! We were a couple! You loved me!" Gabby yelled from Obsidian's back talons. "You just said you were sorry and that you were kind!"

"Me? Love you? HA!" Obsidian barked out a laugh. "I never loved you! The only reason I stayed close to you was to gain information about your group! You would tell me anything I wanted to know about you or your friends. Thanks to you, I know everything about your emotional weaknesses and your past sorrows. Emer and your pathetic Bully Incident; Raider and how his fluffy piece of food ran into the road and died; Paris's tragic story about her father! Ha! Some soldier! Thanks to Gabby's loose tongue, I know about all of you, and I can use it all to my advantage!"

"But . . . but . . ."

"I was never sorry," Obsidian hissed. "And to think you actually believed me . . . heh heh . . . love is so stupid."

Gabby's face went pale. She stared at the ground below.

"Say good-bye to your friend! I know she will bow to me. She will give me her power!" He spread his ebony wings. The wind carried him and Gabby high into the clouds above.

"No! Now what do we do?" Raider asked.

"Transform," Bella said, throwing George's notebook to the ground and putting her right hand on her chest. In a bright flash of light, she was Emer.

Raider placed his hand on his chest, and light flashed around him.

"Paris," Emer said. "Come over here. Ride on my back. Take George's notebook as well. We'll probably need it."

"Got it," Paris said. Emer crouched. Paris grabbed the notebook and crawled onto Emer's back. Emer watched as Paris yanked a piece of yarn out of her pockets and tied it around one of the spikes on her back.

"I'm ready to go," Paris said.

"I'm ready as well," Raider, now Saphir, said.

"Let's go, before any human sees us," Emer said. She launched into the air, spreading her wings. The wind whipped her up into the sky; she soared into the clouds.

"Where did he go?" Paris asked.

"There! I see something!" Saphir yelled, flying beneath Emer.

Ahead of Emer, a black shadow hovered in the clouds. Suddenly, fire shot toward her.

"Look out!" Emer yelled. She flapped her wings, dodging the attack. The fire swept around her. She spread her wings, circling around the black silhouette in the clouds. Saphir followed.

Obsidian flew out of the clouds, watching them with a maniacal smile. His left eye was out of focus and scarred.

"Saphir!" Emer yelled. "Attack!"

Emer dived at Obsidian. She swept her talons at his head, but he dodged and breathed black fire at her. She looped around and dived at him again.

Emer watched as Saphir charged at Obsidian's tail, but Obsidian dodged the attack. Saphir looped around and bit Obsidian's tail.

"OW!" Obsidian roared. He whacked his gem-stone-embedded tail in Saphir's face. Saphir fell a few feet, but he spread his wings and flew around, blood dripping from a cut on his face.

Emer flew by Obsidian's back, gouging her claws into his scales. Obsidian roared, raising his talons and shooting a fireball at her. She dodged it and flew around.

"Seriously, why can't we get any closer to him?" Paris shouted.

"We can't because he has Gabby," Emer growled. "If we hurt him really badly, there's a chance it could also hurt her, or he could do something to her. Clever snake, taking her into his talons."

Paris stayed quiet. "Wait, why are we not attacking because he has Gabby?" she asked.

"Um, because she could get hurt. I care about her, and I don't want her getting hurt."

"We care about Gabby."

"Yes!"

"That's why we're fighting."

"I'd more call it a lack of fighting," Emer said.

"But that's why we fight! Because we care about the Bluescales! Because we care about each other! Because we want to keep all dragons and humans safe! Because we care!" Paris exclaimed.

"Yeah," Emer said, glancing up at Paris. *What does she mean? This is worrying me.*

"That's why my father fought! That's why you and Saphir fight the Bloodclaws! Because you love the Bluescales and you want to keep them safe! It's all out of love! Well, that's kind of a sappy answer, but it's the answer I need!"

"Paris, you okay back there?" Emer asked.

"I'm perfect! Emer, fly closer to Obsidian!" Paris demanded.

"All right," Emer said. "But whatever you're doing, be careful." She leaned to the right, flying over Obsidian.

Suddenly, Emer felt Paris stand up on her back. Emer glanced up, alarmed. "Paris, what are you doing! Sit down!"

"For Father! For the Bluescales! For my friends! For Skye! For Vladmir, for giving me the question! This is all for you!" Paris yelled.

Emer felt the weight disappear off her back.

She watched in horror as Paris fell straight toward Obsidian.

"NO!" Emer exclaimed, swooping down toward Paris.

"WHAT THE—?" Saphir yelled. "What is she doing?"

Emer watched Paris. She was placing her hand to her chest.

Wait . . . is she . . . ?

Bright light flashed around them. Emer covered her eyes, but the light still blinded her.

"What is the meaning of this?!" Obsidian demanded.

When the light died down, Emer opened her eyes. What she saw shocked her.

Paris had become a dragon.

CHAPTER 18

FIGHT AND FLIGHT

Emer watched as a flurry of bright-yellow scales plunged down toward Obsidian's bewildered face.

"Paris! You got your dragon form!" Emer exclaimed.

"Thanks!" Paris yelled back. "I wish I knew how to fly, though!"

Oh no! I completely forgot she has no idea how to fly! Emer thought.

Paris charged into Obsidian. She latched onto his scales, knocking him from his clean hover. Emer dived after them.

"How did she suddenly get her dragon form?" Saphir asked, flying beside Emer.

"Let's worry about that question a little later," Emer said. "Right now, there's a very big chance that someone could die."

Emer watched as Paris and Obsidian tumbled about in the air, free-falling toward the ground. Paris slashed her yellow talons across Obsidian's black scales.

"This is what you deserve for hurting my friends! For all your trickery! You snake-fanged, bat-winged barebelly!" Paris yelled, grabbing Obsidian's ram-like horns and shaking his head.

"LET GO OF ME!" he demanded, breathing a stream of fire at her. She jerked his head away from her. His fire blasted harmlessly out into the sky.

"No way!" Paris said.

"Paris! You've got to let go of him!" Emer yelled out.

"Why? If I drag him down to the ground with me, he'll die!"

"Yes, but so will you!" Emer yelled.

"I'm willing to die if I must to save everyone else!" Paris said.

"But what about Gabby?" Saphir asked.

Paris paused and looked up at Emer. "What's the easiest way to fly?"

"Spread your wings and let go of Obsidian!" Emer yelled.

Paris spread her yellow wings. The wind picked her up as if she were a kite. She dashed straight into the air, flying above Emer.

"Augh, get back here!" Emer said, flying up toward Paris.

"WHEEEEE!" Paris yelled, gliding around in circles. "And you just flap your wings, like this?" She beat her wings up and down, zooming around Emer.

"Yes, just like that," Emer said, hovering in place.

"All right, you filthy Dralerians," Obsidian snarled, flying up to face them. His scales were covered in small cuts. "It's time we talk."

"If you try to fight us again—" Saphir growled.

"No more fighting! Right now, fighting is getting us nowhere!" Obsidian said.

"No fighting? What game are you playing?" Saphir snarled.

"I'll attack him, anyway!" Paris yelled.

"No! Wait!" Emer shrieked. "Don't attack!"

"What?" Paris and Raider exclaimed.

"You want this, don't you?" Emer asked. She reached up by the yarn Paris had tied around her back spike. She grabbed a small, leathery object and held it up.

"My notebook! Hand it to me now!" Obsidian yelled.

"Not until you give Gabby back to us," Emer growled.

"I refuse!"

"You're not getting the notebook, then," Emer said.

"Please! Let me go!" Gabby cried out. Obsidian looked down at her. "What use will I even be to you? You hate me, anyway!"

Obsidian's black eyes stared from the notebook to Gabby, then back to the notebook again. "Fine. Take this girl." He tossed her into the air. Gabby screamed. Emer dived down, catching Gabby in her foretalons. Emer looked at Gabby. Tears streamed down Gabby's face. Emer growled. *How dare this monster hurt my friend this way!*

186

Emer flew to Saphir. "Hold Gabby for now," she said, gently placing Gabby in his talons.

"I will," he said.

Emer flew back over to face Obsidian.

"Well, Emer, you have to stick to your part of the trade! Hand over the notebook," he said, a sly, pointy grin on his face.

Emer looked into Obsidian's black, evil eyes, then to the small notebook she held in her talons. *I can't let Obsidian have this back*, she thought. *I read through this notebook when I was home, suspended. He has written so many evil plans in here. If I gave this back to him, he could destroy us all.*

I know what I must do.

"Saphir!" Emer telecommunicated to Saphir.

"Yes?" Saphir's voice rang in her mind.

"Listen to me!" Emer telecommunicated. "As soon as I say the word 'Now,' I need you and Paris to fly toward the school. Transform into humans immediately. Understand?"

"What are you . . . going to do?" Saphir telecommunicated back, hints of worry in his voice.

"I don't want you getting hurt. Will you listen to the plan I gave you?" Emer telecommunicated to him.

There was a long pause. "All right. I trust . . . you."

"Great. Be prepared."

"You're right, Obsidian," Emer said. "I made a deal. I should stick with it."

"WHAT?!" Paris and Gabby exclaimed.

Obsidian grinned. "Perfect. Glad you're as good and heroic as Demonheart growls that you are," he said, holding out his right talon. "Give me the notebook."

She flew closer to him. Obsidian flew toward her. She held out the notebook in her talon. *Almost . . .*

"NOW!" Emer yelled at Saphir. Saphir bolted away, dragging Paris with him. Emer hurled the notebook into the air. She breathed a plume of green fire onto the notebook. Obsidian's eyes tracked the notebook, now a pile of ashes, as it fell to the ground.

He looked around in fury. He focused on Emer. "How dare you! How dare you!" he roared, lunging at her. His claws slid across her scales, and she winced as they cut into her. Emer grabbed Obsidian's talons.

"You may kidnap people and dragons," Emer said. "You may kill all kinds of creatures. You may come up with millions of evil plans to get your way, but you will never succeed."

She let go of his talons. She swung her talon into the side of his jaw. CRACK! Obsidian roared and then grabbed her forearm. His claws dug into her scales.

"YOU SNAKE-FANGED BASILISK!" Obsidian howled. "DIE!" He smashed his right claw into the side of her head.

Everything went black.

* * * * *

Swirls of color flew about in Emer's mind. Voices echoed in her head.

"The golden age of dragons is upon us!"

"The treaties have been made!"

"The chief's son is hatching!"

The colors swirled around, clarifying to show a bright red dragon egg. It hatched, a red dragon popping out of the egg.

"We shall name him Prodigium!" a large voice echoed in her mind.

What is going on? Emer thought. *These colors, the dragon egg, the dream . . . what is wrong with my mind?*

"It is but a vision, Chosen One," a deep, majestic voice echoed in her mind. "It foretells scenes of the past that shall be key in the future."

How does this dream help my future? Emer's mind yelled at the voice.

"You will know when the time comes," the voice commanded. "For now, rest. Close your eyes and rest, for your battle has only but begun."

Wait, what? What is going on? Emer thought, her mind becoming drowsy. *When will I know? Can you . . . tell me . . . ? Why . . . ?*

The colors faded around her into darkness.

* * * * *

What . . . where am I . . . ? Bella thought. She blinked slowly. The light above shone into her eyes. She squinted.

"You're awake at last!" a voice said. A head suddenly blocked out the light.

Bella jumped up with a start. "Mrs. Medens!" she exclaimed. *The school nurse! If she sees me while I'm in dragon form, I'm done for!*

"Calm down, Bella! You can relax," Mrs. Medens murmured, grabbing Bella's arms. Bella looked at her own arms, which were smooth and pink. *Oh, phew,* she thought, relieved.

"You have to rest, darling," Mrs. Medens said. "You received a really bad concussion. I have no idea how, but you are required to rest and recover. All right?"

"How are my friends?" Bella asked. *Obsidian didn't find them and hurt them, did he?*

"Your friends are doing just fine, sweetie," Mrs. Medens said, brushing a strand of black hair out of her face. "Your friends Gabby and Raider received quite a number of small cuts and bruises. I've doctored them up, though, so no need to worry."

"What about Paris?"

"Oh, the spunky blonde? She received only one bruise!" Mrs. Medens said. "I must leave for a moment to check on Gabby."

"Okay," Bella said, shutting her eyes. She heard the click-clack of high heels and the click of a door shutting.

"Bella? You awake?"

Bella opened her eyes. "Raider!" she exclaimed. She sat up quickly, grinning.

"Shh, stay calm," he said. "I don't want you to become more hurt than you already are."

"Don't worry, I'm okay." Bella grinned. "I've been in much worse scenarios than this. Anyway, what are you doing here? Shouldn't you be in class or recovering in a different part of Mrs. Medens's office?"

"I wanted to see how you were doing," Raider said. "You took quite a nasty fall when Obsidian hurt you."

"Well, I have a concussion," Bella said, looking at her arms. "I also have lots of cuts. So physically, not so well, but otherwise, I'm decent. Do you have any idea how I got back into my human form?"

"No idea," Raider said. "As soon as Paris and I were in human form again, I looked over and saw you falling. I ran over to, well, catch you." He coughed. "And you turned into a human automatically, I guess."

"You caught me before I hit the ground?" Bella asked, raising an eyebrow.

"Well, yes," Raider said, looking away from her. "I didn't want you to be hurt worse."

Bella looked at Raider. "Thanks." Bella grinned. "Did Obsidian leave?"

"Yes. He flew away as soon as he hit you."

"He did? I thought he'd do more to hurt me or, you know, kill me."

"He said he wants to use our power. Think that's why he didn't kill you?"

"I guess," Bella said, "but we have to be careful. He's a dangerous villain, and he isn't afraid to hurt someone for what he wants."

"Well, today he didn't get what he wanted," Raider said. "We stood strong and defeated him."

"True, but he'll be back."

"And we'll be ready."

"Yes." Bella paused, thinking. "You know, I realized something today."

"What?"

"My mother wants me to change, and Lucy mocks the way I am. If I had listened to them and changed myself, I wouldn't have been here to save the three of you."

Raider looked at Bella, a gleam in his eye. "I knew I was right." He grinned. "Admit it."

"You were right. I think I've learned that I'm fine just the way I am. I don't need to change for anyone just because they don't like my interests or habits. I don't need to worry about what anyone thinks of me. I should be happy with who I am."

Raider smiled at her. Bella looked at him. "Well, you learned the exact same thing about an element and dragons." She smirked.

"True," he said. He walked over to a chair and sat down. "You should rest. You've been through a lot."

She grinned, then lay down and shut her eyes. *For now, I am safe. For now, I can rest.* She drifted off into a quiet slumber.

CHAPTER 19

THE GEMSTONE WARRIORS MEET AGAIN

"The meeting of the Gemstone Warriors will come to order!" Emer called out.

"Must you say that at every meeting?" Paris asked, flicking a pebble off her yellow scales.

"Yes, I must," Emer said. "It gets everyone's attention."

"We do have a lot to discuss today," Gabby said. She sat on the ground and adjusted her purple glasses.

"We're running two minutes late," Saphir quipped.

"Saphir, I know!" Emer said, flaring her wings at him.

"Um . . . you requested that we be here?" a voice asked. Emer looked over. Skye had raised his right fore-claw, and he looked confused.

"You seem to just be arguing so far," another voice said. Scalene fluttered and sat down next to Skye. "When are you going to meet?"

"I decided to come as well!" another voice said. "Stonehorn the Cavedweller is here in case anyone gets hurt or wants buffalo ribs or something! Just let me know!"

"Stonehorn, you don't need to follow me everywhere I go," Skye said.

"Anyway, the meeting is starting right now," Emer said. "First on the agenda is to congratulate Skye and Scalene for helping us foil Obsidian's horrible plan!" Emer's friends applauded.

Skye and Scalene looked at all of them. "What did we do?" Skye asked.

"We remembered the Backward-Scale battle strategy and stopped the Bloodclaws. But Obsidian? That new bad dragon? We stopped him?" Scalene asked, raising the purple crest on her head.

"Yes," Emer declared. "When you two figured out the Bloodclaws were going to attack and told me it was a Backward-Scale strategy for Saphir's kidnapping, I figured out it was both a sneak attack and a distracting attack."

"Wait, what?" Stonehorn said. "Please explain."

"Obsidian wanted the Bloodclaw attack to distract me at the Bluescale cave," Emer said.

"Meanwhile, he tried to kidnap me and hurt Raider and Paris at our school," Gabby said.

"However, thanks to you two, we stopped Obsidian and sent him crawling home to his cave!" Saphir said.

"Skye! See? I told you that you could still fight and do stuff!" Paris cheered.

Skye looked at Paris and grinned. "Thanks," he said, then looked closer. "You gained your dragon form?"

"Yeah! Pretty cool, isn't it?" Paris said, looking at her bright-yellow scales and flicking her tail. "It's weird, though, because I have a sapphire on my chest just like you, Saphir."

"You do?" Emer asked.

"Oh, that makes sense!" Saphir said. "And it confirms my theory!"

"What?" Gabby asked.

"A while ago, I estimated that Dralerians' gemstones were based on what month they were born. Emer's birthday is in May, and she has an emerald. My birthday is in September, and I have a sapphire. Paris, your birthday is in September with mine! That explains it!"

"Well, my sapphire is special," she said. "It's not a boring blue, like all other sapphires. It's amber-colored!"

"Really? Sapphires can be that color?" Gabby asked.

"Sapphires come in all sorts of colors," Paris explained. "I read about it in a book in the Bluescale library."

"Paris, while learning more about sapphires is cool, I must know if you have a dragon name, like Saphir's or my name," Emer said. "Do you know if you have one?"

"When my subconscious mind told me, 'Paris, you should turn into a dragon now,' I thought I heard Vladmir's voice saying, 'Rise, Salira, mighty warrior!' So I think it's Salira," Paris explained.

"Perfect! Your new dragon name is Salira!" Emer said.

"Yay!" Salira cheered.

"Wait a minute," Skye said. "This all happened in an environment with humans around?"

"At a school, yes," Emer said.

"How did they react after the fight, when all of you were in human form?"

Salira groaned. "They thought the four of us had gotten into a fight with each other, thanks to all the scratches and cuts we had. We had to lie and say that they were right."

"And because we engaged in 'violent physical actions,' we got suspended for a week," Saphir said.

"I got suspended for another week," Emer grumbled. "The principal said I was not only engaged in a second fight, but I also sneaked into the school when I wasn't supposed to be there."

"That does not sound pleasant at all," Skye said.

"This is why dragons are much better than humans," Stonehorn said. "Emer! You're doing much better with your issues, right?"

"I'm doing much better now," Emer said. "I should ask the same of you."

"I've learned a lot from what happened," Stonehorn said. "I've decided to devote my spare time to protecting—I mean hanging out with—my little brother!" He grinned.

"All. The. Time." Skye sighed. "Are you sure you have nothing else to do in your free time?"

"Nope!"

"Anyway, I'm happy I have my dragon form," Salira said. "Now I'll learn how to fly better. I'll learn how to fight better, and I'll find my element. I wonder what it is!"

"Well, Saphir and I will help you find it," Emer said.

"Saphir will help me find it?" Salira asked.

"I thought he hadn't found his element yet," Gabby said.

"I found out I can summon force fields and protect those around me," Saphir said.

"Cool!" Salira and Gabby said.

"Although," he said, "it still feels like there's something missing."

"You don't need to worry about it," Emer said.

"Emer, when do you think I'll get my form?" Gabby asked.

"You must be patient. Vladmir will decide when you're ready," Salira quipped.

"I know," Gabby said. "It's just that I feel a little left out. I don't have my dragon form yet, and I feel . . . well . . . powerless."

Emer walked over beside Gabby. "Gabby, you're not powerless! Trust me, I know you have strength within you."

"True! You withstood George's temper and stood up for yourself when he kept telling you to get fro-yo with him," Saphir said.

"And you stayed brave when Obsidian held you in his back talons and threw you in the air!" Salira said.

Gabby smiled. "Thanks, guys."

"You're welcome," Emer said.

"So I presume our next plan is how to get the Dark Energy Crystal back?" Skye asked.

"Exactly. We know where it is, though," Emer said. "Obsidian is keeping it in his section of the Bloodclaw cave."

"The only problem is figuring out when and how to get it," Saphir said. "Obsidian will destroy anyone who tries to take the Crystal."

"He'll probably have Bloodclaws around his cave all the time, so it's even harder to sneak in and get it," Salira pondered.

"And he could just trap us and get us to touch the Dark Energy Crystal to turn us evil," Gabby said, eyes wide. "I do not want to be evil. At all."

"Drat, this will be hard to do," Scalene said. "And we have to do it before that Obsidian dragon uses it against all of us. The Dark Energy Crystal, in the wrong talons, could be used to take over the whole world. What if he makes some horrible thing that the Crystal powers and uses it to rule the world and destroy us?"

"Demonheart probably knows by now, too," Skye pondered. "That red demon. I will avenge my father. I will defeat him."

"Skye," Salira said, "you okay?"

His blue eyes focused on her. "I'm better than okay. I am excellent. I know that, despite my injury, I am still a strong warrior who should be feared!"

"Okay, I'll take that as a yes," she said.

"Guys, don't worry so much! I know all of you will figure out a way!" Stonehorn said. "Just give it some time. I know all of you can do it!"

"Yes, we will," Salira said.

"And we'll help!" Scalene said.

"And I'll help from the sidelines with wounds and stuff!" Stonehorn said.

"Yes," Emer said. "It may be hard for us now, but we'll train harder. With two evil dragon leaders out there who have control of an army of wicked dragons and want to destroy us, we must be prepared for battle. We'll fight harder than ever before!"

"Excuse me for asking," Skye said, "but how will the four of you fight Demonheart, Obsidian, and thousands of Bloodclaws?"

Emer looked at her friends, then at him and Scalene, and smiled. "That's why I requested that you attend this meeting," she said. "The four of us decided we needed more help with our 'club.' That is why I'd like to ask if you want to join the Gemstone Warriors and help us fight."

"Me? Be a Gemstone Warrior?" Skye asked.

"You've proven your intelligence," Saphir said.

"You've proven your bravery," Salira said.

"You've proven your determination," Gabby said.

"And we could use more strong warriors," Emer said. "Would you like to join?"

"Yes! I'd be honored to help you take down the forces of evil!" Scalene said, leaping into the air.

"I'd love to! But . . ." Skye looked down at his titanium forearm.

"That doesn't matter to me," Emer said. "You still defeated the Bloodclaw with it."

"I'll join, then!"

"What about me?" Stonehorn asked. "I know I wasn't invited to this meeting and that I'm not a Gemstone Warrior, but . . . is there any way I can help?"

"Well," Emer pondered, "if we need medical attention or food, you could help us with that. Is that all right?"

"More than all right!" Stonehorn grinned.

Everyone cheered. Emer watched her friends, her new teammates. A smile grew on her face.

"We are the Gemstone Warriors!" Emer said.

"Because we're strong," Salira said.

"Because we're smart," Saphir said.

"Because we are not just the Chosen Ones from the Foretelling but powerful dragons with hope," Gabby said.

"Because we're helpful," Stonehorn said.

"Because we're strong no matter our size!" Scalene cheered.

"Because we're determined," Skye said, smiling.

"Because we are friends to the end." Emer looked at her friends. "We will fight against Demonheart. We will fight against Obsidian. We will save the world. No matter how long it takes, we will win!"

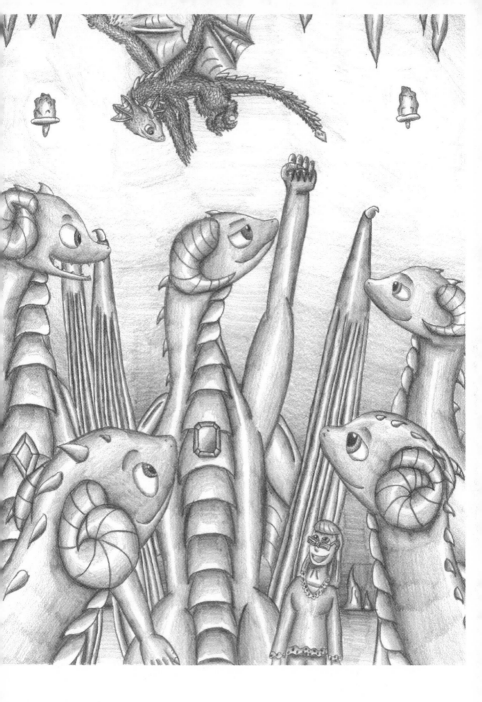

CHAPTER 20

A NEW IDEA

Iridigrarr lay on the stone ground.

His eyes were tightly shut. He clenched his jaw.

Oh, these wounds. Oh, how they hurt, he thought, groaning. He opened his eyes, looking at the large gashes on his red scales. Blood seeped out of the large cuts.

Demonheart was not happy I went behind his back. He reflected back to their conversation.

"What do you mean you left the cave without my permission?" Demonheart had roared at him. "You went on your own out into the human world? How dare you not tell me!"

"Why do you think I didn't tell you? Because you would have stopped me!" Iridigrarr had roared back. "I had Emer within my grasp, closer than you've ever been to hurting her!"

"Fool. Do you realize how many times I've had her within my grasp?" Demonheart had snarled. "I've had her chained up in my cave more times than I can count!"

"You've never had her blood on your scales," Iridigrarr had hissed back. "I've actually had the courage to fight with her!"

"You insolent dracling! You don't speak to your elder that way!"

"You make horrible plans! You're nothing but a worn-out drake!"

"HOW DARE YOU!"

Demonheart had started slicing his claws into Iridigrarr's scales. Iridigrarr had had no time to react before Demonheart had punched him, cut him, and smashed him to the ground.

"This is your lesson," Demonheart had said, his talons smeared with blood. "Choose wisely the next time you go behind my back."

I wouldn't have had to go behind your back if you had just given me the information I needed, Iridigrarr thought, slowly sitting up. *If you had just told me how they looked in human form, I could have gone and brought them into our cave myself. I'd have their power by now. However, you changed my plan, sending Bloodclaws to their school to kidnap them, making any next move around the humans too vulnerable. It is your fault, Demonheart, your fault I had to transform into George to seek their human forms out by sense only. It's your fault I had to try to get them to trust me when they're sworn to another allegiance.* Pain seared through Iridigrarr's scales. *It hurts.* Iridigrarr groaned.

"CAW, CAW!" the crow fluttered over beside Iridigrarr. He crawled up, sitting on his haunches.

"Ah, my lovely pet," Iridigrarr purred, holding out his talon. The crow hopped onto it. "I've decided to call you Poe. It's from a human class in human English! I thought the name fit."

"CAW!"

"I knew you'd like it! You are my best friend . . . my one and only true friend," Iridigrarr said, scratching the crow's head. "You appreciate me, whether I fail or not."

His mind flashed back to Emer. *Emer, that Goody-Two-taloned basilisk!* he thought, hissing. *She foiled my plans! She stopped me from getting her power. She stopped me from getting Saphir's power. She stopped me from kidnapping Gabby and using her power to my will. And she burned my notebook full of plans! Saphir is no better. This wound he gave me means I can no longer see out of my left eye. That Paris girl is an annoying gnat—she cut me so many times! And Gabby . . . stubborn girl, bowing to her friends and not me!* Iridigrarr roared and smashed a nearby stalagmite. The rock shards flew everywhere.

Something caught his eye.

Something was behind the stalagmite. *Ah, my backpack from those days at the school.* He looked at one of the books. *Hmm. Computers. I never did learn much about those while I was there.*

"Look at that, Poe, a book about computers," Iridigrarr said. "It's a machine that's supposed to be able to find all the answers in the world for you." He chuckled. "Nothing can do that."

It really is peculiar to see how naïve, selfish, and boastful humans are. Humans claim to be the smartest animals on the earth. By the Greatwing, some claim to be the only intelligent creatures alive in this very universe. They say they can make everything do things for them. They say they can find new lands, find new animals, make new discoveries. Pfft! Their only power is to invent, to create. They can't sense the weather, their direction, or how others feel on their own. They need their machines. They treat their machines like gods. Why do they need their machines so much when they could just connect back to nature and gain their natural powers back?

Iridigrarr gazed at the book on computers. *They only consider themselves to be smart because they make machines.*

Wait. That's it. Machines.

I should make a machine.

"Poe, go grab my Bloodclaw spine!" Iridigrarr said. Poe flew off. Iridigrarr reached over and grabbed some small pieces of paper and a jar of ink. Poe flew back and dropped the smooth, gray Bloodclaw spine into Iridigrarr's right claw and landed on his left talon.

"If I had a machine, I could scare both the dragon and human population," Iridigrarr said, sketching out a design. "Humans would cower in fear, because something besides a human has made a machine. And dragons would cower in fear, because a dragon has made a human machine. This machine could turn creatures evil, as well as hurt them. Of course, this machine will be powered by the Dark Energy Crystal, because it has the power to turn them evil."

"CAW, CAW, CAW!" Poe flapped his wings in excitement.

Iridigrarr looked at his design. "There! Finished!" He held out his design in front of him and then looked closer.

"Drat! I need a quartz crystal," he growled. "Where am I going to find one of those? The Bloodclaws have no gemstone treasury whatsoever!"

Poe fluttered up from Iridigrarr's talons. He strutted over to Iridigrarr's backpack, pecking out a book.

"A book on human geography?" Iridigrarr asked.

"CAW!" Poe flipped open the book, tapping his beak on a map.

Iridigrarr's eyes went wide. "That's where I can find quartz crystals? In a place called . . . California?"

"CAW!"

"Perfect!" Iridigrarr grinned. "Now, once I gather the supplies, I'll have the world's worst weapon in my control!" Suddenly, his heart sank in his chest. *That's right,* Iridigrarr thought, looking at his red scales, *I have to let Demonheart know about everything that I'll do.*

Iridigrarr thought about it. He imagined Demonheart stealing his machine, claiming it as his own. He imagined Demonheart preventing him from using his own creation. He imagined Demonheart locking him up forever.

I can't tell him about this machine. This machine is my creation. Demonheart will just steal it.

Demonheart will never know about this. I'll lie to him about it.

Iridigrarr snarled. *If only Demonheart were out of the picture. I wish he were gone.*

Better yet, dead.

He laughed a maniacal laugh. "I'll lie to Demonheart," Iridigrarr said. "Then I'll send Bloodclaws out to California through the Bloodclaw Tunneling System underground. I'll make the Bloodclaws gather my supplies. I'll make the Bloodclaws gather the quartz crystals. Then I'll construct my machine. Then I'll kill off my enemies one by one."

Iridigrarr chuckled, then held out his talon for Poe. "Ah, Poe," he said, "Demonheart wants the world to be his, or ours, as he tells me. But, my dear little Poe, the world will not be *ours*."

Iridigrarr looked over at the Dark Energy Crystal. A sudden burst of red lightning flashed from it.

Iridigrarr grinned an evil, pointy grin. "The world shall be *mine*."

ACKNOWLEDGEMENTS

To Mom, for everything. For inspiring me to never give up, to follow my dreams, and to try new things. For motivating me to turn my story into a book. For helping me when I had writer's block. For always being positive and believing in me. For teaching me to work hard for what I want and believe that anything is possible.

To Grandma LaValle for helping me with the very first edits of my book before we even went to the publishers, laughing over the funny tidbits in the story, and teaching me crucial knowledge about writing, grammar, and the English language.

To Papa for helping with my book and putting up with my story that consumed the women in his life.

To my art teacher, Emily Williams-Wheeler, for having faith in my illustrations and encouraging me that I could do it, teaching me important art techniques and skills, and helping me develop my artistic abilities.

To Beaver's Pond Press, which includes:

Alicia, the project manager, for giving me guidance, help, and support along this amazing journey.

Lisa, the developmental editor, for giving me advice on writing and for helping me make my story shine brighter than it had before.

Laura, the copyeditor, for finding all the little things that hid from me that had to be tweaked and for teaching me new facts about writing.

Dan, the designer, for laying out my book, creating an awesome cover, and helping to fix any minor edits.

And to all the people out there who have encouraged me to write, listened to my work, and have big, bright, wonderful imaginations that shine brighter than the stars.

ABOUT THE AUTHOR

Izzyanna Andersen is an eighteen-year-old with a love of dragons. She's been passionate about books and art as long as she can remember and has been drawing and writing small stories and poems from an early age. Izzy began to write and illustrate *The Power of the Gemstones* book series when she was thirteen, and published the first book in the series, *The Power of the Gemstones: Revealing Her Secret* when she was sixteen.

When she is not writing or drawing, she can be found singing, dancing, playing piano, going to the lake, or hanging out with her friends. She currently resides in Minnesota with her mom, two brothers, two dogs, three parrots, and a closet full of dragons.

But secrets can never stay hidden for long; the truth is always revealed one day. For Bella, that day is here.

The adventure that started it all!
The Power of the Gemstones: Revealing Her Secret

Be prepared for what's to come in Book 3...!